THE SONS OF
BATT COLTRAIN

Mike Morris hid the backshot youngster from the posse who were after the outlaws who had robbed the Socorro bank. The Coltrain gang had left their half-brother to die without a grain of conscience — but Pete Coltrain was to survive, and with vengeance on his mind, he took off with Morris's horse one night. Morris set off in angry pursuit, but when he rode into the outlaw camp, he found himself in plenty of trouble.

Books by Amy Sadler
in the Linford Western Library:

A MAN OF TEXAS

AMY SADLER

THE SONS OF BATT COLTRAIN

Complete and Unabridged

LINFORD
Leicester

First published in Great Britain in 1992 by
Robert Hale Limited
London

First Linford Edition
published December 1994
by arrangement with
Robert Hale Limited
London

British Library CIP Data

Sadler, Amy
    The sons of Batt Coltrain.—Large print ed.—
Linford western library
I. Title II. Series
823.914 [F]

ISBN 0–7089–7643–3

Published by
F. A. Thorpe (Publishing) Ltd.
Anstey, Leicestershire

Set by Words & Graphics Ltd.
Anstey, Leicestershire
Printed and bound in Great Britain by
T. J. Press (Padstow) Ltd., Padstow, Cornwall

This book is printed on acid-free paper

1

THE town was quiet, basking in the noonday heat of a sun at its zenith. A hounddog twitched and jumped up, irritated at the fly crawling inside its ear and snapping, thrust a front paw over the ear under attack. The fly buzzed loudly then flew away. The dog turned round a couple of times and flopped down again into the dust beneath a broken wagon near the blacksmith's shed.

Several horses tied at hitching-rails stood hip shot, heads drooping while they snoozed. Occasionally a tail swished away offending flies.

Jordan Coltrain ran his tongue over dry lips and stood up in the stirrups turning to look back at the four men who rode in pairs behind. Pulling a gold watch from his vest pocket he checked the time. They had cut it fine but that might be an advantage. Most of the town's folks would be gone to their abodes for their noonday meals, then they'd take a siesta till the day began to cool. Most of the shops would be closed now. We'll get inside the bank as it's about to close, then work fast and be gone before anyone notices. The manager lives alone, so he won't be missed and the clerk sometimes stops at the saloon for a beer and sandwich, but he won't be missed if he doesn't. All this Coltrain had observed from his two weeks' of patient and casual talk with the locals, when he had worn a false moustache and dressed like a prospector. He settled in the saddle running over it again. A posse would take an hour to get organized. That should give us at least a two to three hours start, maybe more, he thought. All our horses are fresh and done no more than six miles this morning. We'll soon put some distance between them and Socorro. He turned again and spoke. "You all know what

2

to do!" he told the men.

All the riders looked typical ranchers or buyers in their long dust coats. The first two were Coltrain's brothers, Sean and Tim. Behind them was the youngest Coltrain, a half-breed their father had sired with a Mexican girl, and another older man, Jim Warris, a mean, scrawny, dangerous character. Batt Coltrain, who had been their leader till a year ago, had died in a barroom brawl over a year ago. His dying words to Jordan had been: "Take care of Pete." A promise Jordan had kept reluctantly; the brooding youngster nearing eighteen meant little to him or his brothers, and to Warris, who reckoned Pete Coltrain was no better than an Indian, nothing at all; he barely tolerated him.

Pete Coltrain rode with his half-brothers because he had no one else. His mother lived south of the border; he neither knew nor cared where, most likely she was in a brothel by now. He'd been taken away from her when he was barely five years old and had lived amongst the various families who followed the outlaws, who hid out in the San Francisco mountains or the canyonlands when they were not out on one of their raids. He had no illusions that the Coltrains cared anything at all for him. Timothy, three years older than he, was the one he communicated with most. He usually kept to himself though. One day, when he had saved enough dinero he would ride away, probably to California where he could mix freely and be his own man, and not have to take the low jobs such as today, when he would be asked to hold the horses, and be given only a fraction of the haul. As they rode into town Jordan Coltrain turned his big bay gelding in at the hitching-rail across from the bank. The others followed suit. "Pete, you stay here with the horses. If you see anything suspicious, or anyone approaching, especially a lawman, you whistle and get the horses over pronto," Jordan said commandingly.

"Sure, Jordan. I know what to do. I done it plenty times." Pete scowled sulkily.

Jordan took his saddle-bags and went across to the bank followed by the other three. Sean stayed outside at the corner of the building, casually lighting a cigarette.

A tall bronzed man came out from the bank putting a wallet into an inside pocket of a corded jacket. He walked off down the street and turned in at the saloon. Sean wished he was going in there too, as he watched the man disappear. Another man came out from a saddlery shop, locked the door behind him and then got on to his horse and loped away on down the street.

Jordan Coltrain walked up to the counter behind which a youngish man was locking a drawer. When he looked up and saw the Colt .45 pointing at his chest, he gasped.

"Don't bother locking it, just hand out all the notes and put them into this saddle-bag," Coltrain said quietly.

"Warris, you go help that feller in the safe." He nodded at Tim. "Over by the door, keep an eye out."

Shaking uncontrollably, the clerk picked the notes out of the drawer and pushed them into the bags.

A look of pure avarice crossed Jim Warris's face when he saw the stack of notes on the shelves. He jabbed the older man with his revolver, picked up a bag and said, "Fill that and be quick." He laid his gun down on a shelf and started to fill another bag.

As the manager edged along the shelf, his hand slid down to the lower one where a Colt .38 lay behind a box. His hand gripped the butt and he was about to turn when a knife slid into his side. He let out a muffled shriek. Warris retrieved his knife as the man dropped to the floor.

"You finished in there?" Coltrain called softly.

"Yeah, but you'll need to carry a bag under your coat. I'll carry the other. They're both full."

Coltrain gave a brief smile. "Better than we'd hoped. Where's the manager?"

"Inside. Best get moving now." Warris stepped up behind the young clerk and hit him over the head with his revolver. The young man slumped and slid to the floor.

Tim had the door open a fraction watching the street as Warris took some pieces of rope from his pocket and very quickly tied up the young man's wrists and ankles, then put a piece of cloth into his mouth.

Jordan swung the 'closed till 2.30' sign around, took the key and they all slipped out. He locked the door behind them and pocketed the key.

Sean walked casually over to the horse, taking the saddle-bags from Jordan who was holding the bank bag under his dust coat. Pete had the horses ready and quickly they mounted and steadily walked the horses up the street. Only when they were well clear of town and over a rise did they break into a gallup. Warris, at Jordan's side, broke into a grin. "By God, that was one of the easiest we ever done, and I reckon we got us a good haul."

Jordan smiled back. "We'd best put some mileage behind us before we take a rest. It's hot but if we follow the river south they'll believe we're heading down for Mexico. Later we can circle over the river east then cut back and ride due west, make our way back to the hideout."

Sean yelled from behind. "I say we have us some fun. We ain't had none lately and I need a woman."

"That goes for all of us, Sean, only we don't want to be stupid and get ourselves caught. There's a lot of dough here; we can afford to lay low a spell where we won't be found, then play around. The girls back at camp will be wondering what's happened to us."

"I'm sick of 'em all. I say we should go south, maybe down into Mexico and Pete can find hisself a nice Mex girl, maybe he'll want to stay there."

"Sean, I say we go back to camp. I'm the leader; you all agreed when pa got killed. We've done well together, so why push our luck?"

"Jordan's right!" Tim turned to Sean.

"There's something I didn't tell you," Warris cut in. "I might've killed that bank feller in the safe. He had a gun stashed on a shelf so I had to put a knife in him before he could let off a shot. Can't say if he was dead, but I'd guess he won't last long unless he gets help."

"Jesus, Jim! Well, the other one won't come round for a while, and he won't get loose, and he's gagged. Still, I don't like it. It will put a posse on our trail faster. Now we really must get back to the hideout. It'll take two weeks, and we daren't take the train. Damn it!"

"Aw, they ain't going to catch us; we can lay a false trail," Sean said, though he was uneasy now.

★ ★ ★

Simon Brewer felt faint and weak. He called for Crawley his clerk, but his voice was hardly above a whisper. He managed to turn on to his stomach and dragged himself to the safe door that had swung half open. The effort made him almost black out. He was sure he would die soon if the bleeding wasn't stopped. Perhaps Tom was already dead. One more effort and he reached the door.

"Tom," he called. There was no answer. "Oh God, help me!" He managed to get a handkerchief from his trouser pocket and folded it into a wad then pressed it to his side, and once again dragged himself forward and got through the door. The effort caused him to turn dizzy.

Tom Crawley came out of the black depths and groaned. He tried to move a hand but his wrists were tied. Where was Mr Brewer? He pushed himself into a sitting position and swivelled round.

Brewer heard the scuffling sound and gave another feeble call. Crawley heard and with an effort he got himself past the counter by shuffling on his behind. Then he saw Brewer and tried to call out but the gag almost choked him. When he got to Brewer, he could see he was in bad shape, blood saturating his waistcoat and trails on the floor from inside the safe.

Brewer looked up, his eyes fluttering, he could just see that Crawley was tied. With one last effort he got hold of the rope which, fortunately, was fairly loose having been tied in haste. His fingers were like putty and shaky; then the rope came loose and Crawley's wrists were free.

Very quickly Crawley got the gag from his mouth and was working on the rope round his ankles. Soon he was up heading for the door, but found it locked. "Devils locked us in," he snarled. Without further ado he got his shirt off and pushed it under Brewer's waistcoat where the blood soaked through, but Brewer's eyes were closed and a trickle ran from the corner of his mouth. Sweating hard, Crawley picked up a chair and with all the force he could muster, he slammed it at the window which was purposely small and had bars on the outside. The glass shattered and dropped on to the boardwalk. It was then Crawley remembered the spare key in Brewer's desk drawer and ran, cursing himself, to fetch it. He soon had the door open and was running down the street for the marshal's office, his head throbbing from the wound caked with blood.

Duncan Morton was snoozing as he lay on a bunk in an empty cell when Crawley rushed in yelling, "Marshal, the bank's been robbed and Mr Brewer is hurt bad! I'm going for the Doc!" Then he shot out again.

When the gist of what Crawley had said sunk in, Morton leapt up off the bunk and ran to grab his gun belt. He went up the street strapping it on. When he got inside the bank he found Brewer on the floor behind the counter, the safe door open and a drawer hanging empty from below the counter. Quickly he knelt down at Brewer's side, noting the blood across the floor where Brewer had dragged himself. "Brewer, are you . . . Oh Jeez!" He put a hand to the neck. He could feel no pulse.

Crawley came back then with the doctor who moved the marshal out of the way and lifted one of Brewer's eyelids. Then he took his wrist, held it a moment then dropped it. From his black bag he took a mirror and held it to Brewer's lips. The mirror remained clear.

"I guess he's dead all right. Better send for the undertaker. Thank God there's no one to be notified!"

Tom Crawley went to sit on a chair feeling sick and shaken. It had all happened so quickly.

"You'd better let me tend that gash on your head, Tom," Doc said, and pulled a bottle and a piece of cloth

13

from his bag, just as the deputy came rushing in.

Morton called to him to get a posse together. "We'll be going hunting. And tell Jake Chandler we'll be needing him. If he's drunk, pour a gallon of coffee into him. I want to be ready to ride in a half-hour."

Deputy Scranton whistled through the slot in his teeth and took off. The marshal was mad as hell, he could see. Heaven help the outlaws if he should catch up with them. The marshal and Brewer had been friends for ten years or more and often went fishing together. It would be a great loss to Morton.

2

JAKE Chandler came riding back to Marshal Morton. "There's five of 'em. Two hours or more ahead. They stopped on that bluff yonder awhile. Now they're following the Rio Grande."

Morton looked at him. "South?"

"Yep, and they ain't made any effort to hide their tracks, as if they want us to see them."

"I reckon they didn't expect a posse on their tail so quick, and they wouldn't stop to cover their trail till they get well away. I guess they don't know how quick we can get a posse together in Socorro. Now we'll split up. Jesse, you and Herb follow the river north and keep an eye out in case they double back on the other side. When it comes dusk they might easily slip over again, if they do cross. If you spot them, one of you come for us and the other keep track of them and leave a clear trail for us to find."

Morton, in his late forties, had spent his lifetime in the west and knew the New Mexico and Arizona Territories well. He had survived Indian raids, and had done his share of chasing outlaws. Now his good friend Brewer was dead and that made him angrier than a stung bull. There'd been no need for the senseless killing. He pressed his horse onwards in the vanguard of eight reliable men, all of whom had been well acquainted with Brewer. There had been little time wasted in counting the bank's loss, but Crawley, who'd been still in a state of shock reckoned some $65,000 had been taken.

The sky was growing a red-brownish hue to the west and very soon it would be difficult to see riders or the tracks that had suddenly become difficult to follow. Jake Chandler got off his horse when he lost all sign of the five horses' tracks. Cattle had moved over the ground and the fresh hoofmarks and cow pats had obliterated the marks where the river flowed out into a large pool. Jake walked in a semi-circle and found where a fire had been made but it was more than a day old and probably made by cowpunchers. He came back to the river and mounting, put his horse into the water and went across. On the far side he found more cattle hoof imprints and they led away in all directions. A horse had come in from the east and gone over the river, but he found no sign of other riders. After a while he returned over the river. "They're clever. I reckon they rode either up or down staying in the water. They could have gone east but I could find no sign anywhere," he told the marshal, apologetically.

Morton said, "Damn! It will be dark soon! I see no sense all of us going further south if they have doubled back on us." He wiped his brow frustratedly.

Chandler volunteered then, "I'll ride

17

back north till I find Jesse and Herb. The outlaws won't be going towards Socorro again. They must have gone up river and then headed west before Jesse and Herb saw them, I doubt if they've gone south because, from what I hear, outlaws are real good pickings for the bandits who hang around the border these days. I just got a hunch they doubled back."

"Have some coffee first," Morton told Jake.

"Nope, I better not waste any more time. I can get coffee when I catch up with the boys."

Morton and the others watched Chandler disappear into the glare of the sun going down. Jake was a good tracker, as good as any Indian. He'd find the trail again. He was in his fifties, almost bald, but still like a bird dog when off the liquor. Many a young soldier had Chandler to thank for saving his life from the Apaches, but the tragedy was his own wife and child had been killed when Apaches raided his home while he was out scouting for the army.

* * *

From the top of a rise where the five men had stopped to give the horses a breather, Jordan Coltrain could see a small dust cloud a long way behind, and cursed. "They must've found those two pretty damned quick, or we wouldn't be seeing a sign of them yet."

"Aw, we can out-run 'em; in two hours it'll be too dark for anybody to see our tracks," Sean opined.

"Well, I think now's the time to lose 'em. See the cattle down there near the river? Let's cross over then Tim and Pete can go on foot and drive the beeves over our tracks," Jordan decided.

Warris intervened. "Better if we ride up in the river a fair piece. Then we split up, ride east aways and swing back, cross over and ride like hell to the west."

Jordan pondered a moment. "We have to go west to get to the camp. We can ride at night, they can't and torch brands don't help a lot and take time. I'd say there's no more than a dozen of 'em." Jordan had led his small band and kept them out of the law's hands since his pa had been killed. He was shrewd, careful and cunning. Extremely hard and tough, and had known little else but the outlaw lifestyle he had led the past twenty years. He was thirty-six years old, greying fast, had a leather tanned face, and blue eyes that masked his thoughts, even from his brothers. Sean was seven years younger and Tim just twenty-two. There'd been two sisters between Jordan and Sean. One had died and the other gone with their mother when she had left Batt Coltrain after he brought the half-breed bastard for her to look after. She'd been sick of the life, and with one of the men who'd also been tired of the robbing, had simply vanished one day.

If the boys had missed their mother,

they'd not let it be known, but they had blamed the bastard for her going. All of them were hardened outlaws and pursued their wanton ways with vigorous dedication.

They rode to the river and waited in the stream while Tim and Pete, in socked feet, boots tied around their necks, herded some fifty beeves over the hoofprints. Then the two youngsters mounted their horses amid stream and all rode north for several hundred yards before coming out on the east side. Tim and Pete raked out the marks with some small branches, then they split and rode over hard yellow grass.

Pete rode alone, the others in pairs. A half-hour later they all came together under a group of cottonwoods. They sat a while as Jordan scoured the terrain with a spyglass. He saw only cattle along the river banks, some amongst the small bush that grew there. Over the river to the north-west he saw a creek that ran westwards. "We'll get across and follow that creek and head for the mountains. We can hole up there tonight and ride on well before daylight."

"I'll go for that," Warris agreed. The others nodded their assent, and they set off again.

Warris, riding with Sean, looked at him. "I say we split up the dough when we make camp."

"Yeah, let's do that, just in case we get separated."

"All right with me," Jordan concurred. His eyes still searched the plain around them. He was cautious as they came back to the river. "You go over first, Jim, then Sean. Tim and me will come next, then Pete. There's a lot of cover over there so be careful," he warned.

★ ★ ★

Jesse Evans and Herb Brodie had seen the five riders some time ago from where they sat tucked in behind a cluster of boulders and small cedars. "We can get two of them for sure

22

before they get out from the water," Evans whispered.

"What if it isn't them, they ain't wearing dust coats?" Brodie said uneasily.

"They won't be wearing them now. They'll be trying to look like cow-punchers or something. I know it was that big bay tied opposite the bank, and I'm sure that roan was, too."

Evans licked his lips. "I'll take the big one, you take who you like. Then fire at what we can. Best we stick together as we got no time to ride for the others, and we can't miss an opportunity like this. There should've been three of us, at least." He levered his Winchester, rested it on top of a rock and waited. It'd be good to square things for Brewer; it suddenly occurred to him the bank might offer a reward.

Jordan watched Jim Warris cross the river and go up the bank, then Sean close behind him. He put his own horse into the water and Tim came at his left side. Pete stayed back watching the opposite bank a few moments longer. He felt uneasy for some reason. It might be the Indian in him. Often before he'd had such feelings, and with cause. They'd always got away though. Jordan was a good leader, he grudgingly gave him his due. He knew Jordan resented him; he'd once heard him tell his father — 'get rid of that breed bastard, he gives me the creeps'. He pushed the roan into the water and was almost across when a rifle shot shattered the quietness of the growing twilight. He sunk his heels into the roan and it sprang up the bank as more rifle shots rent the air and bullets hit the trees and foliage close to him. He veered right using the cover along the river bank, and saw Tim and Jordan way ahead. Tim turned and let out a yell at him, then something hit him with a thump near his right shoulder blade. He fell over the horn and grabbed it and held himself on. Soon he could see the others bearing

24

left into the plain seeking cover within the short scrub bush. Once they got some distance it would be very difficult to see them. Pete clung on, laying low and in a while the firing stopped.

When Jordan had managed to get off a shot, Jesse Evans took the bullet in his right arm and he dropped his weapon. Brodie squeezed off another shot as rock splinters hit his face and he ducked. "I think I made a hit, the last one. They're gone now. I guess the marshal will be mad, but I can't see what two of us can do. Maybe we should get after them. Jeez, Jesse! I didn't know you were hit!"

"It's gone through me arm, I ain't much use now." Evans said angrily. "The posse can't do much when it's dark. You best go and find 'em, Herb."

★ ★ ★

Jake Chandler heard the gunfire and put his heels into the dun and reached for his rifle. The firing had ceased but he saw movement up ahead. The darkened sky made it difficult to see but he thought he saw horses going west at something of a pace. In ten minutes he came upon Evans and Brodie, and pulled up sharply.

"Jake, it was them, they came across the river. We maybe got one. I sighted on the big feller, but he must've seen something. He ducked and then took a shot at where we were hid. I reckon they'll be hard to find now in this bad light. Is the marshal coming?"

"Nope, he stayed down river where we lost the tracks. If you ain't hurt, Herb, you better go tell 'em. I'll take care of Jesse." Chandler swung down and took a look at Evans' arm. "Good place as any to make camp. I seen they gone west: I'll find their tracks later." He took out his knife and cut away the sleeve of Evans' shirt. When he had cleaned out the wound with river water and bound it up with the sleeve, he got his burlap bag from the saddle horn and got busy making a fire and fixing some food.

★ ★ ★

Mike Morris had just crossed the river when he heard the rifle shots. It didn't sound like someone shooting game, he thought. There were no dwellings for miles. He also heard revolver shots. He hauled his horse in behind an aspen tree and sat listening. The shooting did not last long, then he heard horses galloping away from the river. Briefly, he caught sight of dark shapes melting into the scrub. He thought it might have been someone trying to rustle cattle. "It's none of my business," he told the horse, and patted Nero as he twitched his ears backwards to acknowledge his master's utterings. Over the past two years Nero had become used to the frequent sharing of Mike's thoughts. They had ridden the range cowpunching, and had recently come all the way from

Montana. When his master got down to refill his canteen, Nero slurped up water and took advantage of the break and cooler air.

* * *

When Pete Coltrain fell off his horse he hit the ground hard and the horse, suddenly unburdened, let off a buck or two and surged forward to catch up with Tim Coltrain who was riding wide of his companions. On seeing the empty saddle he let out a yell.

Jordan turned to look across, and seeing the riderless horse next to Tim's, he hauled in on his bay causing Sean, riding behind, to almost pile into him. Then suddenly he heard a crash behind and a loud oath from Warris as his horse went down on its knees, and he only just managed to get his leg out of the way before it fell on its side.

"Oh goddamn it! My horse must've been hit," Warris shouted as he scrambled to his feet.

"Sean, you go back and look for Pete," Jordan took command. "Tim you catch up Pete's horse."

"We can't hang about here long," Warris snarled. "I can ride with Tim, he's the lightest. We'll buy or steal another hoss tomorrow some place."

Sean came back looking worried. "Jord, Pete's been hit, he looks bad."

Jordan cursed and went off with Sean. They'd seen no sign of the posse coming for some time, but he was sure they were out there somewhere. When they got to Pete he got down beside him where he lay prone and struck a match shielding it in his hands. "They got him in the back. See if he's got a pulse, Sean."

Sean swung down and put a hand to Pete's neck. He could feel a faint throb. "Naw, I reckon he's croaked."

There was an almost inaudible moan, a slight move.

"He's still alive." Jordan looked hard at Sean just as Warris and Tim arrived.

"Is he dead?" Warris asked eagerly,

sitting on the roan as Tim got down.

Sean said, "I reckon he will be soon. Been back shot."

"Then I can have his horse." Warris grinned. "We'd best be moving on, there's no telling how far behind the posse is. Now you don't have to give him a share, neither."

Jordan, who'd been thinking along those lines, gave Warris a withering look. "See what's in his pockets, Sean, then let's get going."

There was little of any consequence, and Sean pocketed the few dollars he found. "Ain't worth toting him any place to bury, it'd only slow us down," he said and got mounted, and followed the others at a lope.

Had it been Tim or Sean, Jordan would have taken him. There might have been a chance; he'd seen men survive such wounds. He put his heels into the bay. In an hour or so they would be into the mountains and safe for a few hours, he figured. His conscience bothered him some, but only on account of the promise he'd made to his father, not on account of his bastard. How could he have been so sure Pete was his, anyway?

Pete Coltrain only vaguely heard his brothers come and look at him before he passed out again. Later, it was cooling fast as his eyes came open. He felt the pain in his back, heard a nightbird call as he lay with one arm under his forehead, the other under his body. When he tried to move he felt blood ooze into his shirt and lay still again. He found it difficult to arrange his mind to focus on what had happened. When he moved and tried to put weight on his right arm it sent a scorching pain through his back under his shoulder-blade. Then a sound came from behind him like a hoof striking a stone. His breathing was difficult as he lay possum thinking about lawmen. Then he began to worry he might get trod on by cattle, or that a coyote might find him. Someone was humming softly, he heard leather creaking and a horse snorted, then a rattle of gear. He ran his tongue round his lips and called out, feebly, "Someone, help me!"

Morris pulled his horse in sharply. "You hear anything, Nero?" he asked the twitching ears. Nero blew down his nostrils again and put up his head. Mike lifted his Colt and sat listening.

A voice was calling in a whisper, some yards ahead.

"Help me, please!"

Very slowly Mike got down, dropped the reins and went stealthily forward. Guided by the moaning sound he came to the shape lying in sand near a bush. Easing over carefully, wary of a trap, he pointed the Colt at the form. "You there! I have you covered! Don't try anything, Just stay still."

"Mister, I'm hurt bad. I need help," the voice came weakly. "Oh God, help me!"   Still holding the gun on the man, Mike looked closer and could see the arms were covered by the body. Either hand might have a gun or a knife, he thought. Pulling out a match he struck it on a stone and saw the dark mark on the jacket. He put the Colt away. This must have to do with the shooting he had heard earlier. Who had shot him and why had he been left behind?

"Listen, I'll have to build a fire so I can take a look at you. Can you hear me?" Mike asked.

"I hear you, please hurry, it hurts bad."

Moving quickly, Mike tied Nero to some mesquite, then cut some short bushes with his knife and built a fire, and very carefully moved the man on to a blanket close to it. He could see now it was a lad with thick dark hair. He wore western clothing and some very good boots. Mike didn't give much for his chances, the bullet would be lodged inside somewhere. When he got the jacket and shirt off he could see the wound had coagulated. Even if he could get him to a town, the riding would likely kill him, and he couldn't see properly in the dark to probe for the bullet.

The lad moaned.

"You seem to have been back shot," Mike said. "What happened?"

"Some men hiding in some rocks shot at me. Please, mister, can you get the bullet out?"

"I'm not a doctor, and all I've got is a wide blade knife, I might kill you if I tried."

"I'll die anyway if you don't help me."

"Your horse, it must have run off." Mike told the youngster. "Or did it get taken by the shooter?"

"I don't remember," the lad murmured and drifted into unconsciousness.

There seemed little Mike could do so he made himself a meal and then took out his mouth-organ and played it softly for a while before he rolled up in his other blanket.

It was nearing first light when Morris was awakened by voices and bits jangling some distance away. He got up quickly believing it might be the men who'd shot the lad. On an impulse he gathered up the brush he'd stacked for the fire and placed it over the lad, wondering if he was still alive. Unless anyone poked around they would not see him. He also put the saddle and his gear in front of the brush and moved away to the other side and away from the burnt down fire, then got under his blanket again. Nero would be sure to whicker when he heard the other horses.

Jake Chandler halted his horse when he spotted the dark shape near the mesquite and heard it snort. He held up a hand and the marshal came alongside him. "I can't believe they'd stop here," he said, puzzled.

"Only one horse," Morton answered. "Probably a traveller, or a cowpuncher. This isn't the trail."

Chandler nudged his horse over slowly, carefully.

A voice told him to, "Hold it right there, I have a gun on you. That's no way to come busting into a camp."

"Mister, there's at least six guns on you, so you best ease that gun away real quick, or you'll regret it." Morton's voice came loud and clear.

"The gun's in its holster. Now what the hell do you want? I haven't anything worth stealing 'cept my horse and if you take him, you're low down, mean critters," Mike said acidly and got up.

"We're lawmen." Morton stepped forward to take a close look at him. "Who are you, and what's your business here?"

"I'm just travelling through. The name's Morris. I heard gunfire yesterday so I got off the trail. It might have been robbers; there's plenty of them about, and a fella can't be too careful," Mike informed the group of men and moved further away from his blanket.

"You see any riders yesterday, 'bout sunset?"

"Yep, I was over the river, but it wasn't easy to see against all that red. Was some riders moving west."

Morton grunted. "You better be careful, we're after some bank robbers and they done murder!"

"Well, I'll be moving on soon as I've had breakfast. I'm on my way to Arizona. I hope you catch 'em," Mike said affably.

Chandler came back after poking around by the horse and Morton got mounted. "Sorry to have disturbed you," he threw at Morris and joining the others they rode off as the sky became lighter.

When the posse came upon the dead horse about a mile further on, Chandler was thoughtful. There were a lot of hoofmarks coming and going, but the posse riders had ridden over the ones going back to where Mike was camped.

Morton checked the horse and saw where the bullet had entered its chest. "Sure came a long way before it caved in," he said to Chandler.

"There's four sets of hoofmarks now, but I don't see any as looks like they carries extra weight." Chandler looked puzzled. "They might have buried someone but there's no sense us wasting time looking. If he's dead, that's it."

Brodie called out, "Jesse said he was sure he hit one of 'em. I reckon we better get after them varmints real fast, now we seen their tracks."

Morton swung into the saddle. "Let's ride then," he yelled and they set off after Chandler who was already way ahead following the tracks like a bird dog.

After making sure the posse had ridden well out of sight, Mike piled some brush on to the fire and got it going again, and then he took a look at the form under the blanket. The body was warmish, though the air was still quite chill, and the lad was still breathing.

"Well, I'll be doggone! This boy wants to live! I must help him — give him a chance," Mike told himself. "For all I know he might be one of the bank robbers. I reckon his buddies left him to die, and him a youngster. That sure is mean."

He gave Nero a drink from the canteen, then got coffee made. After drinking two mugsful, he took the knife from the lad's belt and placed it over the flames. He had seen a bullet removed before, and helped hold the man down, but it wasn't a pleasant chore.

As he rolled the lad over, he groaned, "Hombre, that hurts!"

Mexican, Mike thought. Probably why they left him. I sure hope that posse don't come back right now. The blade had cooled so he began to probe by the light of the fire and the growing dawn. The wound bled and Mike sweated from nervousness and the heat from the fire. He could feel the boy tensing, see his fingers digging into the sand. He had guts. The pain must be sheer hell. He gave a silent prayer. Don't let the boy die.

After some fifteen minutes the knife

tip went under the bullet and Mike lifted it out with two fingers. Grinning he wiped his face on his sleeve. Sure hope he don't bleed to death. He went to fetch his towel and cut it into strips, but before he bound up the wound he heated his own broad knife then placed it on the flesh for a moment.

The lad yelped and fainted away, and Mike got him bound up and put a clean shirt of his own on him, then lay him down on his left side and covered him up.

In a while, after a smoke, Mike made breakfast. What the hell am I going to do with the lad, he wondered, if he survives, and I give him maybe a fifty-fifty chance. He needs a doctor, and I need supplies. I reckon I'm stuck with him for now, he mused worriedly.

3

NERO lifted his muzzle out of the creek as Morris put the top back on his canteen. He had ridden over to the creek and left the youngster covered under some bushes. Anyway, Morris thought, I'd figured on a day's rest for Nero. It would be some time before the lad would be able to take the jolting on the horse, if he survives, and only then at a walk. He swung back into the saddle and rode quickly as the day began to warm up. Noting jack-rabbits and prairie chickens, Mike knew his next chore would be to go hunting. The fire had burnt down and he leapt off Nero and went to the form under the blanket. Still breathing evenly, thank God!

He got Nero unsaddled and hobbled, leaving him to browse, then fetched more brush for the fire and placed the coffee pot on it. While he waited for it to boil he pulled out a mouth-organ from his vest pocket and played a tune. Mike Morris didn't mind being alone particularly. At twenty-five years of age, he had spent a considerable time wandering the lonesome trail. When he was only twelve years old, his father had been killed in a coal mine in Pennsylvania. His mother had later married a sanctimonious, penny-pinching, railroad clerk whom Mike had hated. At fifteen, he had run away from home in search of an uncle who worked on the railroad, and who took care of him then. Mike's uncle, Henry Morris, had never married, though he loved women, and the whiskey bottle.

Mike's thoughts drifted to the past. His uncle had loved to travel and when he had saved $1,000, he had slapped Mike on the back. "Let's go see something of this big country," he'd said, in great good humour. Unfortunately, Uncle Henry had been parted from a tidy piece of his savings in a poker game in a Kansas cowtown, and there he had taken another job to recoup his loss. It was there that tragedy struck, when an over-keen sheriff had arrested Henry Morris for horse theft. The sheriff and his posse hanged Morris from a tree, refusing to listen to both his and Mike's pleading that Henry had had nothing to do with the horse-stealing. It had been a terrible shock to Mike. Even when they found out they had hanged the wrong man, there was little sign of remorse. Some sympathetic men in a saloon where Mike helped clean up each evening, had a whip-round and Mike paid for a proper burial for his Uncle Henry. He'd been eighteen at the time and had even thought of taking his own life. But he had drifted from place to place picking up jobs when he could. Eventually his pain had subsided and he'd become a cowpuncher in Montana.

When Mike came upon the youngster, he was on his way west with a vague idea of reaching the Pacific Coast. This had been something his uncle had hoped to do, and perhaps ship out to South America. In Montana, Mike had left a girl behind who had tried to rope and brand him to a life of domesticity. It was not what he wanted. "Stay free, Mike," his uncle had told him. "Never owe money. Keep your nose clean, and don't expect too much from life, then you won't be disappointed."

What would Uncle Henry have done with this youngster? Mike wondered. He'd've looked after him, that's sure. If the lad was one of those robbers, what had driven him to become an outlaw? Aw heck! I'd best take him some place and leave him. He's not my concern. I can't waste too much time, and I need more provisions.

Picking up his rifle, Mike walked off moving silently amongst the brush. In the sand patches he saw rabbit and bird droppings. A hundred yards further on he saw a jack-rabbit which ran off. He shouldered the rifle and

44

fired. The rabbit rolled over, its belly throbbing, legs kicking, then it lay still. Picking it up Mike walked back to his camp. No sense in getting more right now; too much rifle fire might attract attention. Might be some of the posse men returning, or a cowpuncher about. He would have to construct a suitable story as to how the Mex got backshot, if anyone came upon them. Trail bums, that might do. A bushwhacker had tried to jump them. What if someone recognized the Mex as one of the bank robbers? Still, he didn't look really Mexican, he might be one of those immigrants from Italy or some place like that. He had blue eyes for one thing.

What the hell am I doing, Morris checked himself. I don't want to be tied in with him. I'll just say I found him if anyone should ask, and that's no lie.

After he had eaten half the rabbit, Mike rolled himself a cigarette and sat leaning on his saddle in the shade of a mesquite. Nero had also sought shade and stood dozing.

Pete Coltrain stirred then moved an arm to flick away a fly from his nose. He lay on his left side, a blanket covering him. He could feel the sun's heat burning through. Memory came to him. Had he dreamed it though? Someone had found him when it was dark. He moved and let out a yelp as a pain shot across his back.

Morris sat up quickly, his well-worn stetson slid off his face. He must have fallen asleep. Well he needed it. Getting up he went over to the boy and found himself being stared at with puzzled eyes. "So, you've come round. How do you feel?"

"Plenty bad, *señor*. It hurt *muy* — like knife!" Why he had lapsed into the silly Mexican talk, Coltrain wasn't sure. Mostly he had tried to forget it, wanting to be a real Americano like his father and brothers. It might be a good idea though. Yes, pretend he was Mexican, come up looking for work and someone had shot at him. "You take bullet out, *señor*. Now I remember. *Muchas gracias!*"

"Do you think you could eat something? I have rabbit. It's best you don't drink too much, you bled a lot."

"*Si*, leetle bit rabbit, leetle bit water!"

Morris lifted the saddle over and very carefully lifted the lad so he could sit against it with his left side, so as not to press on his right.

Coltrain gritted his teeth and Mike noticed the pallor below the deep-tanned skin. He fetched a tin mug and helped Coltrain drink a little, then he gave him the piece of rabbit stuck on a stick.

"What do I call you?" Morris asked.

Coltrain hesitated. "Pietro Alvarez," He moved then and gave a shout. The effort of eating and sitting caused him to sweat, in a lot of pain.

"Well, Pietro, last night a posse came to my camp just after I found you. I covered you with brush so they wouldn't see you. Don't ask me why. Anyway, it seems they were chasing some bank robbers. I have no real liking for posse men, so what I did was on the spur of the moment, you understand?"

"*Si, comprende*," Coltrain said and lapsed into silence.

"You want to tell me how you got shot?" Mike asked.

"I think somebody shoot at me from rocks." That was no lie, Coltrain told himself. Why should he explain?

"I heard gunfire when I was on the other side of the river, and I saw men riding away as the sun went down. When I found you there was no sign of your horse."

Coltrain suddenly realized his holster was empty. Either this *hombre* had taken it, or Jordan, or maybe one of the others. He put a hand to his shirt pocket and then realized it was not his own. Now he had no horse, no gun, and the few dollars he'd had were gone. He'd best not rile this stranger, he might have his horse stashed some place, and maybe had his gun and money. "The *hombre* who shoot me, he take the *caballo*, I guess. Good thing you find me, *señor!*" Coltrain said, and tried to smile.

"You'd be dead now if that bullet had stayed in you. Beats me how you survived. You'd best get some rest. You ain't out of the woods yet. When you can travel, I'll get you to a town, or homestead or somewhere. Until then it will be jack-rabbit and beans till they run out, or a bird. The water is four miles away."

"You will stay with me, *señor?*" Coltrain said incredulously. "You do this for me?"

Morris observed the boy closely. "Can't leave you here, no horse, no anything! You'd die! But I reckon there was someone who hoped you would. Had the posse found you I reckon they would have buried you here."

Again Coltrain said nothing. He

closed his eyes. It crossed his mind that the *hombre* might hope to collect a reward on him. If he went off to get the law, a coyote might get at him while he slept. That's why he was staying till he could take him to a town. He's no fool. Bitterness swept over Coltrain as he remembered more of the voices. Warris saying, 'He's croaked', and Sean going through his pockets. They'd gone and left him to die. Didn't even consider taking him along till he did die, so they could, at least, give him a decent burial. The posse had dropped behind, they had the time to take him. Then, if they had, it would have killed him. Well, I know where they're heading. I'll find them, then I'll kill them, all of them! Coltrain drifted into sleep.

It was dark, much later, when Coltrain felt a presence beside him. He was still propped against the saddle. His left hand slid to his belt searching for his knife, but he felt weak and his head throbbed.

"It's all right, *amigo*, it's Mike. Listen, I've seen a firelight west of us. It might be some posse men on their way back. They'll wonder why I'm still here. How do you feel? Can I move you to another place?"

"Not so good, *señor*, the pain is bad."

"I thought if I got you on to my horse, we could walk slowly and get over to the creek, there's more cover there and better shade, and I might get a duck tomorrow. Nero will lie on his side and you put a leg over, then he'll get up."

When he saw the dark shapes of the trees along the creek bank, he stopped and got down. Coltrain had come round again and held fast to the horn. The moon was up and showed Morris a dry wash running to the creek so he led Nero down into it and stopped near some *piñon*. He got Coltrain down and lowered him into some sand, then covered him with a blanket.

Very quickly he unsaddled Nero, tied him to the trees and collected wood and got a fire going. He was not himself particularly cold, but he was worried about the lad: he'd lost a good deal of blood. In a day or two he should have produced more. If he lived through the night, he thought his chances were quite good.

★ ★ ★

It was three days since they had moved to the wash and Morris was feeling rested, though somewhat anxious. Twice he had ridden away leaving Pietro covered under some bushes at the edge of the creek, after three men appeared from the west, and he felt sure they had seen him. He was on the far side of the creek when they came up to him, just as he was stalking an antelope. They passed the time of day, and gave him some cigarette tobacco. After they had gone well down creek, he went back to the lad. For two days he had been in and out of consciousness, often raving and throwing the blanket off him. He muttered names such as Jordan, Warris, and something about water, a cave. At first Mike had thought he was raving about The Bible. Then there were more names, and threats about killing them. But now he was through the worst and mending, though the wound looked ugly and festering, which worried Mike. If it went poisonous, that would be very serious.

The sky was clouded with a hint of thunder in the air as he came back with a sage-grouse. A lot of meat and nothing much else was pretty darned monotonous. His sugar was finished and there was only enough coffee for one day. They must find a settlement, or a ranch where he could buy provisions — and what he wouldn't give for a beer, Mike drooled.

The Mexican was sitting propped against a tree bole, in amongst its roots. He looked up quickly when he saw Mike approaching from behind some willows. The man was good at avoiding trouble, he thought. Was he also on the run? He said little about himself. He still felt unsure about him, though he had been kinder than anyone had ever been to him since Batt Coltrain had been killed. His father had often given him a beating, but then brought him a present after one of his raids, such as the horse and the knife. Where was his horse now, and who was riding him?

"*Señor*," he greeted Morris, "the knife you take from me. You did not leave it behind?"

"Nope! I got it in my saddle-bag. You were not in any state to be having it these last few days," Morris said, then he took the knife from his bag and gave it to the lad, rather reluctantly. "Quite a handy weapon." He smiled and looked into the eyes that he often found regarding him in some sort of puzzlement.

"When you go off and leave me, I need something. I have no gun, maybe you take that, too?"

"Never saw one. Whoever left you must've taken it. I think tomorrow we must try to find a town or a place to buy food, I'm all out of everything. And you need a doctor to look at the wound. Could be poisoned. I've got nothing that will help."

"We best ride at night. Then you go in and get what you need. It is not possible I go to town."

"Listen, Pietro, maybe it's best we find some Mexican folks, they could help you."

"Why, Mexican? I'm not Mexican, I'm American, same as you," Coltrain spoke angrily, his accent gone.

Mike gave him a hard look. "Then why talk in that pigeon Mex? You have a Mexican name, though your eyes are blue, but that don't say you ain't Spanish."

"My name is Pete; the other, it is better you don't know. I'm grateful you helped me. I guess I can look after myself now, only I have no money, nothing!"

"You need to see a doctor. I'll get you to a town and give you some money. Then I have to make tracks," Morris said, deciding the matter.

They ate the bird which was bitter, and drank the last of the coffee. "Why do you rob banks?" Morris asked quite suddenly, taking Coltrain off guard.

Startled, he didn't answer at first, then he shrugged. "I was born in Mexico. My father took me away when I was five, from my mother. He came to see her when he was hiding from the law. He was killed over a year ago, and my half-brothers let me ride with them. They always treat me like a kid, make me hold the horses, and they liked to call me a half-breed. They left me to die! For that I will kill them!" Coltrain snarled.

"Then why don't you ride on and find a new life? You'll only end up on the end of a rope, or breaking rocks in some hell pit for the rest of your life. You're young; your life ahead of you. Besides, how will you find those who left you behind to die?"

"Oh, I'll find them! I know where they are heading! After I do what I have to do, then I ride on."

"You're going after those brothers, then? Jordan, Sean?"

"How do you know their names? Who are you?" Pete looked hostile and angry.

"You talked in your sleep, *amigo*, when you had fever," Morris said, disarmingly. Then he brought out the mouth-organ and played softly till it got cold. He got up and built up the fire and pulled his blanket over him.

Coltrain also lay under his blanket, but he did not sleep. It was a long time till first light. His mind was busy and he was tense, the wound throbbed and burned. The night was well on when he slid out from under the blanket. He took his boots and the blanket and tip-toed up the wash. The bridle hung on a branch of a *piñon*. He reached for it then went up on to the grass where Nero was pegged out.

The horse nickered softly as he went to it and quickly slipped on the bridle. Then folding the blanket, he put it on Nero's back. After putting on his boots he tried to leap up on to the horse, but a pain shot through his back and he dropped to his knees. After a moment or two he managed to get Nero down and put a leg over and the horse got up, snorting.

Some stars were out but the waning moon was almost hidden by cloud as Pete kneed the horse away along the creek bank, heading west. He swung out away from the creek later and came back to it a couple of miles further on. A thread of guilt ran through his conscience as he rode. It was cold, and to lope was painful, so he had to let the horse walk. Now Mike had no horse. He would probably not wake for ages. If he did, he'd not notice anything till he got up, but he might do so to put more wood on the fire, then he would surely see he'd gone.

When the false dawn was upon Pete,

he was riding down a slope and saw dark shapes across the creek. Ranch-house and buildings, he grinned. There will be a saddle somewhere about, he felt sure. Closer in he left Nero tied to an old plough some distance away from a barn. He didn't want him snorting and nickering at other horses that might be in a corral. He went round the corner of the barn, wishing there was a bit more light. To his relief he found two saddles on some rails and lifted one quickly. By the time he got back to Nero, dragging the saddle, he was almost done in. After he got the horse saddled, he stood for a while, sweat running off his nose end. Then he put a foot in the stirrup and with difficulty got into the saddle, the pain so bad he almost fainted. After it subsided, he pointed Nero to a track running north and by the time it was daylight, he could see, almost a mile ahead, a cluster of buildings. A settlement, or a small town. He must get something for the pain, but he had no money. He would have to find a way, perhaps there were some Mexicans he could ask for help; after all, he still knew the lingo.

4

RESORTING to profanity was not Mike Morris's way, but he let out a string of oaths when he found his horse was gone. At first, when he woke up and saw Pete wasn't at the other side of the fire, he believed he must have gone to relieve himself. Then he sat up abruptly on realizing the blanket was not there, but he might be feeling the cold and kept it round his shoulders. He got up and found some wood and got the fire going, and still there was no sign of the lad. Quickly he strode along the wash and noticing the bridle was gone from the branch, he rushed up the bank. He knew then he'd been fooled. Well, the lad did say we should go in the night, only he forgot to mention he was going alone. After I let him know I'd guessed more or less who and what he was, I reckon he took fright. "Damn it, he's not getting away with stealing Nero! No sir, he's not! I'll find the damned thief if it's the last thing I do!" Mike growled and went to put his things together.

Carrying a saddle and gear was no easy task while walking on rough ground. By God he was quiet; I never heard a thing, Mike thought. I was damned tired, though, looking after him all this time. After all, I did save his life. To leave me afoot not knowing how far we were from any place. How mean can a man get? I should've known better than trust him. He could've killed me after I gave him back his knife.

★ ★ ★

A couple of cowpunchers looked him over from under their hat brims, as Mike approached the corral where they were working some horses. He put the saddle down with relief. "Mind if I help myself to water?" He nodded towards a water-trough by the barn, sweat pouring off him.

"Sure, you look kinda beat," one man said. "You lost your horse?" he enquired.

"Yep, woke up this morning, he was gone. Maybe five or six miles back. You got one I could buy?"

"Got some fresh broke mustangs; you a range man? You looking for work?" a tall thin man asked him.

"Nope, I'm travelling through. I could use some grub though if there's any to spare," Mike grinned.

The foreman came down the yard then and took Mike to look at several horses in a small paddock. "You say your horse is gone — you got any idea how? It ain't likely it just up and ran off, is it?"

"No, I guess he was taken. I'll need a bridle as well. I'll take that bay, he looks like he can move."

The foreman and the others laughed. "Oh he can move all right, up, down and sideways. The skewbald would be a better choice. Someone lifted a saddle off that fence last night. I reckon he was your thief. If you catch up with him, the saddle has DP on the flap. Maybe you can send it back somehow; it belonged to the boss and cost over a hundred bucks."

Morris smiled. "I'll try to do that, if I do find whoever it was. How much for the bay and a bridle?"

The foreman gave him a questioning look. "You can have that damned back-breaker for $45, including the bridle."

"That seems fair," Morris said and peeled the amount from a small roll of notes and handed it over. "I'm real obliged."

"Bad thing taking a man's horse, leaving him afoot. Lucky you were not too far from water and this ranch — it's still a fair distance to Puertocilo," the foreman informed Mike, then he asked him to stay for the noonday meal, hoping to learn more about the stranger.

After eating a good thick steak with potatoes and greens, some peach pie, followed by coffee, Mike was on his way after thanking the foreman and his wife for their hospitality. They had learned little from him.

He was sure that Pete would have headed where he could get food, and perhaps a doctor. He would steal the food, and probably hold the knife on the doctor while he dressed the wound. On the other hand he might have fallen off Nero and be lying almost any place.

The bay went well enough, but had at first raised its back, and Mike had put his legs into it and let him run for a while. A horse knew well enough from the beginning how a rider would treat it. It also knew how much a good rider would let it get away with, and who was going to be the boss. Mike soon showed the bay.

In Puertocilo, Mike first went to the saloon, a rundown shack-like place where some men sat idling away the hottest hours, some Mexicans amongst them who gave Mike appraising looks from under their straw sombreros. He tethered the bay to a rail and went inside and asked for a beer then took it to a rough table and got the weight off his blistered feet. The beer wasn't good but it was wet and he drank it down and ordered another. If only he'd not met that youngster and still had Nero, he would not have a care in the world. Now he had to waste more time searching for Nero, he couldn't just abandon him like that.

There was no sign of Nero in the street, then he had not expected to find him there. That boy was in a hurry to get some place, and it was almost certain when he found his brothers they would kill him. Well, that isn't my concern. I gave him a chance once, now he's on his own. Morris's thoughts ran on.

The store, he was told, opened again at 3.30, but, "If you're in a hurry, Gilman will come down and serve you, he lives over the store."

"I'll wait; it's too hot to travel now. Is there by any chance a doctor here?" Mike asked, but wasn't at all hopeful. No doctor in his right senses would put up his shingle here, he thought.

"Ain't no doctor, but there's a veterinary fellow who looks after the ranchers' stock, and he do take care of folks with cuts and colic and such. Good as any doctor, I'd say! You be needing a doctor?" the barman asked Mike.

"Yeah, I got blisters on my feet." Mike suddenly thought he could get something for them.

"He lives up the street, turn left at the top. Set back a piece, you'll see his house. Usually a buggy outside, if he's in."

"Thanks, I'm obliged." Mike left his empty glass and strode out and went up the street. He found the house with the buggy outside, and he tethered the bay to a wheel and went to knock on the door. In a few moments it was opened and a tall, lean man appeared looking over a pair of half-frame spectacles that sat on the end of his nose. He had thick white hair, sharp features and looked as if he spent his time out in the scorching sun of the desertland.

"Can I help you?" he asked looking at Mike in a pleasant manner.

"It's me, I have blisters on my feet from walking several miles. The barman said you might have something."

"Surely, come on in. Looks as if it might thunder, I can feel it," the man said conversationally.

Morris followed him into an office that was full of shelves with bottles and boxes on them. In the centre was a scrubbed pine table, and in a corner a forlorn looking dog looked up from a basket where it lay with one of its legs bandaged.

Morris pulled off his boots, then the socks that needed darning and a good wash.

Andrew McKenna whistled. "Not a

pretty sight. How'd you get in such a state?"

"Well, I was camped way back some miles, and someone took my horse in the night. I walked to a ranch and they sold me another horse."

"Thought I recognized the bay. So, Ballan managed to dump that razor-back on you, did he?" McKenna said looking amused.

"Nope, I picked him out. He's a good horse. You just have to let him know who's boss."

"Well, I'll be darned. Broke a few folks' bones that horse has." McKenna gave Morris another searching look.

"I got him cheap, and I don't have much money to spare. I'll sell him when I get my own horse back."

"What was your horse like?"

"A sorrel with a white blaze and one white sock, at the left hind leg."

"You got any idea who took him? Did you shoot at any person?" McKenna asked as he dressed the blisters.

"Nope, I was sleeping, I'd been

riding a long ways. I was dead tired, or I would have heard."

"A youngster came in this morning. He was in bad shape and looking for a doctor. Said he was bushwhacked some days ago. Said someone took a bullet out of him. Was vague and he was riding the sorrel you just described. Rather a strange story, I thought. The wound was festering so I got it cleaned out and stitched it up again. It's a miracle he could ride like that: the pain must have been awful. He had no money, but I couldn't have done *nothing* for him. I told him he shouldn't be riding for at least another week. He took no notice. Just thanked me and left."

"You know which way he rode out?"

"He asked about the trail to Arizona and Flagstaff. That's at least a two-week ride — more in his case. He might never make it!" McKenna said shaking his head.

"Do you happen to know if The Hole in the Wall is anywhere in that region?" Mike asked casually.

"I did hear the outlaws' hideout was in the Faibab, then there are a lot of places to hide in that region. You figuring on riding all that way?"

"I'd ride to hell and back to find Nero," Mike said, a hard, set look on his face.

McKenna had vanished through a door and in a few moments came back with some new socks in his hand. "You can have these, my daughter keeps me well supplied."

Colouring, Mike asked how much he owed for his treatment, and fished the $1.50 out from his pocket. "I'm much obliged."

"There's a map in my living-room showing the routes across Arizona, you can take a look if you like. But if you think your thief is heading for Flagstaff, I'd be inclined to back track towards Albuquerque and get the nearest train stop. You could even wait at Holbrook, as I'd say he'll most likely head up that way to take the west trail." McKenna threw in the sound advice.

Mike took a look at the map and made a rough sketch of the trails and watering places. He was, on reflection, not in favour of riding in such heat across the desert terrain. The outlaws would more than likely head for a town to spend some of the money they'd stolen, and they might chance the train having lost the posse. Pete would also be heading in the same direction, and he would be clever enough, if he hadn't fallen off somewhere and lay dying, to cover his tracks. It would be a lot easier on the bay if I take the train and wait for him to show. If he don't then I'll have to ride on, Mike decided.

5

THE posse had halted north of the Mangus range in the Rocky Mountains. Jake Chandler had just caught sight of the outlaws who appeared to be camped on a high plateau at an old log cabin. He quickly went back to find Morton.

"They probably think we've quit by now." Morton turned to the other men. It was just on dawn and chilly, where they had camped overnight under a rocky overhang.

"Let's get after them." Morton swung into the saddle. "How far up are they?" he asked Chandler.

"A half-hour up a game track." Chandler pointed to the narrow winding path he'd just come down.

The Coltrains were striking camp as Morton and his six men came spread out on foot, using rocks and the sparse timber for cover. Yesterday they had ridden hard across North Plains after leaving the Salado River. Once the outlaws were over the pass, they'd be into Arizona Territory in less than two days, Morton knew, and out of his jurisdiction. It would not stop him if he thought he could catch up with them. He needed to get to a telegraph office and send word ahead. Three of his men had gone back, the others were already talking of quitting. This might be their last chance to try and capture, or maybe kill, one or more of the murdering scum, Morton thought. He caught sight of Chandler pumping his arm. It was the signal. A shot rang out from his right where Don Whipple was located. Chandler began firing and Morton saw puffs of smoke coming from near the cabin and fired at the spot. There was a burst of firing and bullets whanged off rock and hit the pine over Morton's head. Horses snorted and he saw a man scrambling upwards and fired, but he missed and the man ducked for cover.

Jordan Coltrain was tightening the cinch of his saddle when the bullet cracked over his head. He whipped his rifle from the scabbard under the saddle and ducked behind a boulder. From below he caught sight of a puff of smoke and saw at least three figures scrambling amongst the rock and undergrowth. He fired quickly when he saw a hat, then he shouted at the others who were still inside the cabin, "Get the hell out of there before you're trapped."

Sean went out of a side window and got to his horse behind the cabin. Warris and Tim came legging it round the corner as bullets hit the cabin with loud thuds.

Jordan was firing rapidly at points where he saw a flash or puff of smoke. Sean got to him and fired while he reloaded. The possemen were unable to get in closer as there was an open space at the front of the cabin. A couple of them were trying to work their way up at one side and Chandler at the other side was firing up at Jordan.

When Chandler stopped to reload, Warris and Tim, with the horses, ran using the cabin for cover and got to some small boulders then followed a track used by bighorn sheep. Bullets spanged off the rocks, then Sean and Jordan were firing again keeping the posse busy till both Warris and Tim and the horses were in behind a group of boulders. They started firing and Jordan and Sean crawled upwards till they managed to get in behind the boulders. Then again, in pairs, they went upwards using every bit of cover. The first pair firing continuously, holding the possemen at bay till they were all out of rifle range. The strategy worked well, they had used it before. An hour later they were moving through the pass out of view.

When the Coltrains made it to the big boulders, Morton and his men went back for their horses. It was no use trying to follow upwards if their mounts were left way below. It was a bitter moment when they knew the outlaws had got over the top. When they came up over the crest there was no sign of riders. They followed on downwards using an old Indian track, now little used.

By nightfall, having stopped only for water and to give the horses a breather, the four outlaws were in sight of a group of dwellings. While Sean and Warris watched their back trail, Jordan and Tim went to see what they could purchase. When they returned to the wash with only a small piece of sidebacon and two tins of beans, a homesteader had sold them, the four of them were not well pleased.

"Should've got off earlier this morning, then we wouldn't have left the vittles behind," Sean grumbled. "That damned posse must've had a good tracker and they sure must've come on fast."

"It's just about a day's ride to the Arizona border that farmer said. Then we can head up for the trail to Flagstaff. Four or five days we should be heading for the mountains and home," Jordan said hopefully.

"I'm for a rest in Holbrook and some relaxation," Sean mumbled as he spooned beans into his mouth with his skinning knife. "We'd best try and shoot us an antelope tomorrow, or jackrabbit, I'm starved."

"We can't afford to underestimate that posse. They'll figure we'll follow the wash west, there ain't nothing north but the Zuni Reservation, and, who knows what south, and I'd bet that sheriff will be sending telegraphs when he hits a town as got wires, if he ain't already got one of his men to do that from Socorro. But he won't have been in touch again to say where he's heading. We can't risk letting too many folks see us." Jordan was adamant.

★ ★ ★

The posse was well into Arizona when they rode along the dusty street between a row of adobes and one or two clapboard buildings. They were dejected, grimy, parched and tired. There was only a small store-cum-changing station for the staging line, so they swung down in silence and tied the horses to a rail in front of it. "This is as far as we go," Duncan Morton told the weary men. "We did our best. They had good horses, and we'll not catch them now: they could have gone in any direction." The men nodded and trooped inside and sat down at a long bench table where two men sat eating a mess of stew.

The storeman's wife came forward. "You wanting the cooked meal?" she asked looking them over without interest.

"Whatever you have: we're quite hungry, and if you have beer we'd like that now," Morton said.

While they were eating a four-horse stagecoach came rattling to a halt in front of the store sending in a cloud of dust. The teamster and two passengers came in and sat at the end of the table.

When Morton got into conversation with the teamster after hearing they were heading for Holbrook, he asked the man if he would take a telegraph message for the Holbrook sheriff to send out where he thought best.

"I'll pass the note to my relief when I get to the next stop, as far as I go," the man offered obligingly. "Be there tomorrow."

Morton got up and went to buy some tobacco for his pipe which he had not had time to bother with for days. Tomorrow they would set off again for the long ride home. There was nothing else they could do.

* * *

Although Mike Morris had lost several days taking care of Pete and had ridden almost back to Albuquerque to find a train stop, he arrived in Holbrook ahead of the outlaws. He was acting purely on a hunch. Taking the train had cost him, and he was not overly endowed with the ready. All told, he had about $290, his horse and a change of shirt and underwear. It had cost him $45 to buy the horse and that was aggravating, to say the least. He had a fair degree of stubbornness in him, though, so he was not about to give up on finding Nero. He did not waste money on a hotel, but slept in a hollow near a river that ran in from the Painted Desert. He'd never before seen such country, such vivid colours. The sky at sundown showed glorious hues that had him just standing completely awestruck. Perhaps he would stick around for a while, anyway.

It was while Mike was having his breakfast that he heard voices, and one in particular sounded angry as he was protesting loudly, "Jordan, I might as well be a monk if I don't get me a woman soon!"

Pete had mentioned Jordan in his feverish ravings, Mike remembered and got his gear packed up quickly. Staying in the wash where he'd camped, he shadowed the four horsemen, feeling an excitement within. When he could see the horses more clearly he took note of the large bay and big man in the saddle, also the dun and roan. He was more than convinced these men were the outlaws, and Pete's brothers.

A short way out of Holbrook, two of the men halted in a grove of cottonwoods, and Mike had to make a detour to avoid detection and to follow the other pair into town. He watched them head straight for The Pleasure Palace.

By mid afternoon a heavy rain storm swept thunderously across the plains and Mike headed for the livery stable where he took refuge up in the hay loft. It was voices and guffaws that woke him much later, and he was sure they were the same he had heard earlier in the day. Keeping very still he lay listening as the two men collected their horses which they must have brought in out of the storm.

"Jord and Tim will want to come on

in for sure, when we tell 'em about that Pleasure Palace, Jim."

"Ain't nothing to stop 'em and they'll be a mite wet I'm thinking. Do Tim a heap of good. Sure is one hell of a Pleasure Palace, Sean! We'll pay another visit later, eh?"

The two men led their horses out and Mike watched from the hay window as the skies were clearing, and the air came in with a new freshness.

As Mike scrambled down the ladder, he was quite sure now that those two were Pete's brothers. He had heard the names, Sean and Jordan, and those were the ones Pete had mumbled in his fever. He took himself off to the café and ordered coffee and pie, then watched the street. The sun was on its way down when the big bay and the dun came in from the west. They tied up outside one of the saloons and the big man and the younger one went inside. In a little while, Mike also went into the saloon and casually headed for the bar where he ordered a beer. He sipped it slowly as he raked his eyes around the room and saw the two sitting at a table; each had a large beer before him. It was easy to see they were related, in fact he could see a strong resemblance between the younger one, and Pete, when he came to the bar and stood quite close to him. He ordered two more beers and two large whiskies, and Tim Coltrain looked directly at Mike as he put the drinks on to a tin tray and collected his change.

Mike gave a brief smile. "Thirsty weather," he said, realizing he'd been staring at the young man, and turned away to pick up his beer glass.

Through the mirror, Mike saw the big man look his way when the other sat down and spoke to him. Shortly afterwards he left and went to seek the shadows of a hotel wall where he could stand and observe the saloon. He hoped he would not have long to wait. If they followed the other two's course of action, he figured they would be heading for the Pleasure

Palace pretty soon. It was something he had been contemplating on doing himself, but he wasn't keen on such places. His thoughts dwelled on the girl back in Montana for a while, and his conscience smote him. Well she'll've gotten over it by now, he thought. For almost a half-hour he waited, feeling the chill in the air through his thin jacket. Then the two men came out, and as he had thought, they headed straight for the Pleasure Palace, where there was liquor, gambling and women of all shapes and sizes.

If only Pete would show up he would get Nero back and be done with the whole lot of them. He didn't wish to kill the youngster though, especially after saving his life. He felt proud of that, but to take a man's horse, and leave him afoot in that dried-up country, was as low as a man could get. The boy had bitter anger in him, that Mike knew. Youngsters were given to do thoughtless and reckless things. He knew himself about that. He had been bitter for a long time after seeing Uncle Henry hanged by those thoughtless men. The best way to find Nero might be to follow those men when they rode out. Another day they had said. They might change that. It'd be best for me to camp out there somewhere in sight of them, just in case, Mike decided. I could wait here for days and Pete might never show up. He knows where they are heading, so he'll take the shortest route. One thing in his favour though, they won't be expecting him. Oh hell! What if they should shoot Nero? Bastards like them won't hesitate, if they catch him following them. I better be real careful myself. That young one, he'll remember me, Mike told himself.

Taking the westerly trail, Mike kept riding steadily for some time till he thought he saw the glimmer of a fire over to his right. He was about two to three miles out from town and circled off the trail to go northwards of the spot where he had seen intermittent flashes, as though from a camp fire. Placing his gear up-wind of the camp which he could see now was within a semi-circle of short cedar trees, Mike used a shallow dry wash. After he had pegged the horse out, he then walked off quietly, his rifle in his hand, to go and take a look. When close enough to smell the fire, he got down to belly crawl till he could hear voices. It came to Mike then that he ought to have gone to the sheriffs once with his suspicions about these men. The posse surely must have given up long ago, it was out of their jurisdiction. There would likely be a reward for the outlaws. If he did go to the sheriff, he'd never find Nero. Not if Pete was going straight to the hideaway. No, he must follow the men, see where they went, then afterwards he might consider telling the law. He might be on the wrong scent; his task was difficult.

"Listen, Jim. When we get back to camp, you pick out another horse from the wild mustangs. Pa bought the roan for Pete. I reckon Tim should have it. Pa paid quite a lot for it. It'd be best it stays in the family."

Mike drew in his breath sharply and strained his ears, his heart beating like a sledgehammer, at what he heard.

"I don't think so, Sean. I think I'll be keeping him. I rid him this far, now he's mine, he's used to me."

"Jordan will decide, he's the boss," Sean Coltrain said.

"Not over me, he ain't. Nobody gives me orders. Batt never tried it, and Jordan better not," Warris snapped.

"Jordan's the leader; he done us good figuring out where to hit, and how to do it. Him and me took risks checking out that bank in Socorro. You done all right by us Coltrains, so you better ride if you ain't satisfied."

"Oh, jest shut up, Sean! Get some sleep. Might be we'll go back to that Pleasure Palace again tomorrow."

"I don't think so. We best not push our luck."

Mike moved back carefully till he could stand up again. He'd heard enough. The fourth man was not a brother. He now knew their name — Coltrain, that's what Sean had said. He was beginning to know these men he'd become bound up with. The big one was Jordan, their leader. That figured. He was the oldest, though the one called Jim was almost his age, too. The roan belongs to Pete, and he will want him back. It gets harder, Mike thought. If Pete sees that one riding his horse, he'll see red and go in there like a young raging bull. I don't give much for his chances. He'll be sure to find himself a gun afore he shows; most likely steal it like everything else.

During the night, Jordan and Tim returned to the camp somewhat noisily, and the sounds carried clearly to Mike where he lay. They appeared to be falling about over gear, and a sharp admonishment and several expletives were exchanged before they all settled down to sleep.

"We're leaving first thing," Jordan had muttered before pulling his blankets over him.

Mike was ready and packed up, after eating a cold breakfast, and watched the four men heading out towards a river that he'd been told was the Little Colorado. If he hadn't been here trying to find his horse, he'd most likely have been riding over some dried-up desertland a lot further south. It was beginning to look greener now and by evening they had ridden past two settlements. Two at a time, the men had gone in while the others stayed back out of sight. But they rode easily, seemingly sure they were no longer being followed. They were north of the river now and although in some desertland, there were mesas and terraces of land showing colours of yellow, red and mauve, and a pinkish purple haze in the changing light. There were Indians, too, walking along a trail, with coloured blankets around them. By God, Uncle Henry would've loved this,

Mike thought, sadly.

Mike had no idea how far the outlaws were going, but the veterinary had said that outlaws hid in the mountains near a big canyon. Mike had heard of the big canyon and had believed the men who spoke of it were inclined to exaggerate, but McKenna had seemed impressed by it. When he got done with his searching for Nero, he might just go take a look at it for himself. The following day the men crossed the river again at a settlement, where it ran east. They later camped for the night in a wide valley and Mike could see mountains on just about every skyline. In the morning they were following a valley between large timber forests. Down a shallow ravine water trickled from the higher plateaux. That evening Mike gathered wood and cooked a meal, tired of eating cold food. He felt apprehensive now, believing the outlaws were nearing their camp. They seemed to be taking more precautions, and once they almost came back on him before he got out of sight by scrambling down a crack in the land. Mike wondered if they had seen him.

Once he had looked back during the day and thought there was another rider on an opposite ridge. It was open land, anyone might be riding across it. There were cattle in the valleys, and he had seen some horses running upwards into the timber. So far he had been lucky in avoiding being detected. They would be watching their back-trail very carefully now, if they were heading for a secret place. He wondered, too, just how far behind young Pete was, and if he was, in fact, heading this way. He hoped he was, but hoped he would find him before he went busting in there to confront his brothers.

The bay had turned out to be a good horse, he would probably keep him and use him as a pack horse when he had something worthwhile carrying. The Pacific Ocean seemed a long way off now and he wondered if he would ever make it there. Perhaps he should find a job for the winter in Arizona on one of the ranches, or he might try around here, it was a pleasant place to settle, he thought. Feeling reasonably safe hidden well within thick timber, Mike rolled up for yet another night, on a bed of pine needles, hoping that there were no wolves or cougars in the vicinity.

6

THE day following Pete Coltrain's visit with the veterinary, he was paralleling the trail heading north-west, keeping it in sight, not wishing to meet up with travellers. He had no wish for company. His most urgent need, however, was food which he'd been unable to obtain in the small town. The saddle he had stolen fortunately carried a canteen and he had it full of water. All he had eaten since absconding from the wash with Nero, was a small portion of jackrabbit he'd saved from his last meal with Mike.

The wound felt much less painful since the treatment, and he had a small bottle of laudanum the vet had given him after directing him to use it sparingly, or he would find himself falling out of the saddle. There were jackrabbits and sage-grouse a plenty, and Pete cursed his brothers who'd taken his guns, not to mention his horse. The heat through the middle of the day was too fierce so he sought shade and managed to get some sleep till it cooled. By the third day, after missing a jackrabbit with his knife, he was almost in a state of delirium till he came across some sheep and with great effort, taking the riata from the saddle he attempted to slip a loop over one of them. After three tries he was successful, and Nero stood as though he was back on the range with a calf at the end of the rope. Pete got down and slit the sheep's throat as it lay bleating loudly, and Nero snorted at the strange smell disapprovingly.

It took Pete ten days to arrive eventually at Holbrook — a distance of some 200 miles. After living off the mutton for two days he encountered a drummer heading south and with whom he made camp for the night, sharing his meal and listening to his endless chatter. Long before dawning Pete had gone several miles north, taking with him a Winchester rifle, shells, matches, frying pan, coffee pot, sugar and a bag of coffee all liberated from the drummer's wagon.

During the heat of the day he rested and rode in the cooler hours. He shot rabbits and prairie chicken, and spent a night with a Mexican sheepherder who fed him on tortilla and beans. His condition had improved considerably. The wound itched from the stitches and the laudanum was all used up, but the pain had decreased to a dull ache.

At least Pete knew now he would not die and his thoughts turned to revenge on his brothers. He also watched his back-trail in case the man Mike might come boiling up behind him in a rage. He was convinced Mike would probably buy a horse at the ranch from which he had stolen the saddle. He felt some guilt over Mike. He had saved his life, taken good care of him like no one had ever done before. Maybe they could have been friends, *amigos*. But he must do what he had to do. That was what he must concentrate on now.

When Pete came to Holbrook it was dark but he did not ride in till the night was well on and he was sure the townsfolk would all be abed and asleep. It did not take him long to force his way into the main store through a window at the rear where he lit a lamp and after finding a sack, he helped himself to levis, warm shirts, a thick wool jacket, a .44 Colt, more shells, cigarillos, whiskey, beans, dried fruit, sidebacon, cheese, canned peaches, more coffee and sugar. The sack was heavy and bulging as he made his way back to the rear and lifted it carefully over the sill and placed it on the ground. The lamp was extinguished so he climbed out and carefully closed the window. Within fifteen minutes he was well away from town, the night cool and overcast. He grinned and rode on and when the dawn came went down into a split in the terrain. Tethering Nero to some bushes he set about making a fire and cooking himself a good breakfast, then he rolled up in his blanket and slept till the sun got to him. Once again he set off facing a north-westerly wind and by midday he was forced to take cover behind some boulders as a storm swept across the plain bringing tumbleweed, loose sand and heavy rain. After it had passed he found the going more difficult, the ground soggy and by nightfall it was quite cold in the first throes of fall. Pete felt tired, but soon he would reach the mountains where the outlaws hid out in the summer months when they weren't out robbing or on a spree of debauchery and spending. Those who were not caught or killed came back to the camp they thought of as their home. Mules were used to pack in provisions for those who remained in the hideout, or for the outlaws to buy from a store which was run by an older outlaw retired from his wild and wanton life. In the winter months when the snow began to fall, they all moved out to hide in a canyon further south, or disappeared over the border for a change. There were wild mustangs to be caught and some men spent time rounding up what they could to sell to the army.

As he rode, Pete was thinking of his brothers. If he killed them he would be alone. They had left him to die; they did not want him; they deserved to be killed! He had his money hidden, almost $10,000, the amount he had aimed for, then he would go, that was what he had decided. He could buy land; live where he pleased; move where no one would know him, not that he was known as his brothers were. No more robbing, no more hiding, running from the law. No more living in the mountains with nothing to do but play poker or visit the girls in the cat-house. He would be like Mike, go where he pleased. Was Mike running from the law? He had said he had no time for lawmen. What if he was a wanted man? Hell, why did he keep thinking about him? He'd been kind though. We could have been *amigos*.

By the next day Pete was nearing a small canyon he was familiar with. At the far end of the narrow valley was an old shack. He rode along a goat track through some pines and came up behind it and got down near a rickety corral and tied Nero to a rail. He caught sight of José Garcia leading his burro laden with pieces of wood. The older man came up with a welcoming smile.

"*Buenas dias, José!*" Pete called to him.

José left the burro by a lean-to. He returned the salutation. "Is cold now at night. Winter come early, I think. Soon I will move down near Sedona; this time I stay," he told Pete.

"When the time comes I will help you move the sheep and goats. First I have something to do," Pete offered.

He lit a cigarillo and gave one to José. He had found this valley one day quite by chance. The outlaw camp was over to the north of it beyond some peaks. He had often visited the older man when his brothers had left him behind when he was younger, and his father had said he was not old enough. He enjoyed José's company; he did not ask a lot of questions, and he invited him to share meals with him.

"You stay?" José looked at him, noting the loss of weight. "You no look so good, *amigo!*"

"*Si*, I stay, maybe a day or so. I am very tired, I ride a long way. I will sleep now. You look after my horse for me."

The man nodded as Pete entered the shack and after taking off his boots and jacket, threw himself on to the wooden framed bed in a corner. In a few minutes he was asleep.

When Pete woke up several hours later, it was dark. He sat up and struck a match on the wall. He saw Garcia asleep sitting in a chair, his head on the table. He smiled, got up and went outside. When he returned, José was awake and had lit the lamp. "You sleep good, *amigo!* You feel better now?"

"Yes, I feel better. You take your bed now. I will make some coffee."

As soon as it was light José was up and tending his goats and sheep while Pete made breakfast. After they had eaten he delved into the burlap bag and brought out a pair of levis and a shirt. "These for you," he said and handed them to José. José took them. "*Muchas gracias,*" he said with no hesitation. He knew the boy would not give them to him if he could not spare them. His own trousers were worn and thin; the new shirt he needed badly.

After breakfast, Pete took the rifle. "I'll get us some deer meat," he said and went up the slope behind the shack. If he had a father like José, Pete thought, how different it could be. Always he felt at peace with Garcia, the man who asked no questions, accepted him as he was and shared his home and food willingly. After he got his own horse back, he would get his money from its hiding place in the cave. He would bring one of the mustangs for José as a parting gift, after he had helped him move his flock. An hour later he returned to the shack with an antelope and sat watching José skin it. Afterwards he got his shirt off and asked José to take out the stitches from his wound. The process was extremely painful: they should have come out sooner. José fetched a bottle of tequila from a shelf and wiped the wound clean and let Pete drink half a mug full, then he slept again.

When Pete woke again, it was another day. He heard José busy with his axe; sheep bleating. He got up feeling almost strong again. He did not wish to rush things. He must have a plan, and he needed to be quite fit. He decided to go and fetch his money first and leave it with José. If his brothers should see him and by some chance, kill him, then José could have the money. One by one he planned to kill them, make it look like an accident, that was how he would do it. He drank some coffee, ate a piece of cheese then taking the side-gun and rifle went off up the slope till he found a place almost a thousand feet up from the shack. He was sweating even though it was cooler at such a height. The Colt, he noted, fired a fraction to the left. The Winchester was fine. Before he went back down he shot a two-pronged antelope and a wood turkey.

Two days later Pete rode out the way he'd come in. "I'll be back, maybe tomorrow, there is something I have to fetch that I would like you to keep for me, José."

Garcia watched him ride away. That boy is heading for trouble. He has anger inside him. Perhaps he seeks the one who put the bullet in him, Garcia thought. He'd heard of outlaws who hid up in the mountains. Nobody knew just where. He was sure the boy was one of them. Once he had been laying traps over the other side of the ridge and had heard gunfire far off. A posse had spent days in the mountains and forests searching, but they'd found no one. They had shot one of his sheep and eaten it. He had been very angry, as they had given him nothing for it. He called his dogs and went to check on his flock, still wondering about the boy. Sometimes he seemed almost Mexican, he spoke the language in a queer sort of dialect. His eyes were blue like the sky, and without the moustache he looked Americano, but there was something about him. At times he came and went like an Indian. Then those who rode the outlaw trail were careful men. He might be a half-breed.

7

WHEN the posse was preparing to set off back for Socorro, Jake Chandler decided not to go with them. He was free to do as he pleased; his small house would come to no harm and Marshal Morton would look in on it now and then. It didn't particularly matter where he laid his head down. He believed he could still do something about those outlaws. To rob a bank was one thing, but to murder the manager was downright mean, he thought.

Morton felt he would be wasting his time but wished him luck and gave him a $100 note to tide him over; he was still sworn in. "There's bound to be some reward money and you'd best look in at any law office you come across. Give them any help about what the outlaws look like, what they were riding. They'll be feeling safe now; could be more inclined to go into any town they hit. They got a lot of money and they'll be itching to spend some of it!"

Chandler felt sure the outlaws would hesitate to cross over the Apache Reservation, and his conjecture appeared to be right when he learned from a farmer that two men had asked to buy food off him. One had been riding a deep red horse, the other, a good looking roan. He'd also seen two others hovering back in some timber. They had all ridden off together, moving northwards. He figured they were most likely heading for Holbrook.

A good feeling inside him, Chandler headed straight for Holbrook. Unhampered by the posse, he made good time and arrived there in two days. He went first to the sheriffs office to check through a pile of warrants. There were posters on several outlaw gangs. One drew his attention that mentioned the Coltrain Brothers, wanted for bank raids, and various other robberies and murder throughout Colorado, Wyoming, New Mexico and Arizona, thought to hide out in the mountain region north of Flagstaff. Sheriff Dowling gave Chandler a few ideas, naming the San Francisco Mountains and the Kaibab. "You'll never get in if they're using The Hole in the Wall, not that you'd be wanting to do such a foolhardy thing," he said looking at Chandler thoughtfully. "There's always snipers in the mountains, I've had three men lost that way. Only thing we can do is hope to catch those renegades in the middle of a raid somewhere."

"I might just try and find where they headed then hang around a while; they have to come out some time. My guess is they won't stay up there when the snow comes," Chandler gave his opinion. "I'll head for Flagstaff, that must be their nearest source of supplies. I know the horses. We hit one man and we found a dead horse, but never saw if they'd buried anyone, nor did it look as if one of the horses was carrying extra weight. That puzzles me."

"Well, I wish you luck," the sheriff said. "If you need any help in Flagstaff, go see Bill Procter, he's the sheriff there. You tell him I said, hello!"

Chandler figured he was probably a good four days behind the outlaws. He had slept almost round the clock after calling in two of the saloons, trying to gather any useful information. One man said he was sure he had seen a big man on a tall bay horse. "Was with a younger man and they looked like they was brothers, I'd say. You ain't the only one as been asking questions. A feller got off the train, day or so ago, was kinda close-mouthed, wanted to know things but wasn't saying much hisself, if you know what I mean. Acted as if he was waiting for somebody."

Chandler ran that bit of information around in his thoughts. He forgot to ask the man if the stranger had had a horse with him. It might be he was the one who got clipped. If so, he must've walked a hell of a long way to the railroad, or, he might just've picked up a horse some place. He was sure he was on the right trail now, sure those varmints were heading to the mountains north of Flagstaff. Thing was, how in hell was he going to find them?

Discarding the idea of taking the train, Chandler set off following the trail to Flagstaff. He might just pick up some more bits of information on his way, and he might find out if they left the trail at some juncture.

Three days later, Chandler came into Flagstaff. He was thirsty, bone weary from all the riding, and he went into the first saloon that met his gaze. He sank two pints of beer then went to put his horse away at the livery barn. By the time he had found a rooming-house he was ready to drop. He simply threw his gear on the floor, took off his boots and dropped on to the bed.

Having slept the clock round,

Chandler got himself cleaned up some, then partook of Clara Nolan's good food. Then he went to see Bill Procter, and told him about his intention to find the robbers.

"You've come a long way. I did have a wire from a Sheriff Morton. If that gang came this way, they'll be holed up now in the mountains, probably for a few weeks. They'll move out when the bad weather comes to warmer places, and spend the money they got on booze, women and gambling. Then they'll start all over again, robbing and killing," Procter said frustratedly. "$65,000 is a lot of dough, and that is what they took in Socorro. If I had that kind of dough, I'd buy me a ranch." Procter sat shuffling posters around. "The gangs who hole up north of here don't come into Flagstaff, so they won't be recognized. Some mustang hunters come down to sell the wild ones they catch. They sell to the army, and most of the men are older. We think they may be part of the set-up, the men

111

who've given up robbing, the ones who stay back in camp to look after things, and they have women with them. It would take an army to comb the canyons and plateaux up in that region," Procter informed Chandler.

After consulting with the liveryman, and an old prospector, Chandler put enough food together for several days. A trail ran due north which he took and later angled slightly west towards some peaks he could see reaching a fair height. He was reminded of days gone by when he had been trapping in the lower Rockies region. The colours here, he thought, were as good as any he had seen. When the sun had swung round to the west he was traversing a long slope and pulled up at a spot where the trees had thinned. He had spotted a rider on a bay horse who was sitting looking upwards. Chandler clicked his tongue, and excitement stirred within him. On further observance through a pair of binoculars, he was sure it was not the tall one he had hoped it would be. The man was intent on something, however, and he decided it was worth investigation.

★ ★ ★

The bay nickered as Morris patted it on the neck. Well he had one friend, at least. The horse was inside a corral which was behind a long cabin situated on a high plateau. All around the grassy meadow were steep slopes ascending to rocky peaks. The slopes were timber covered till they met the rock. On one slope a mass of dead tree boles lay as if they'd been suddenly torn from their roots by a great storm or a massive landslide.

Morris was in a pensively unhappy state. He had trailed the Coltrains, believing they had not seen him. They had followed a creek into the foothills of the San Francisco Mountains, then taken a narrow game track that had wound up through a forest of pine, interspersed with sycamore, aspen and elder. He had stayed well back, catching infrequent glimpses of the horses' colour. The scenery was magnificent with the fall tints. There was fresh snow on the peaks. The trail had led up and down and they had crossed a bridge made of tree boles which the bay had found slippery and treacherous. Most of the afternoon they had crossed the east side of a long slope always moving higher and Mike had lost track of them: all of a sudden they were gone. He believed they must have covered their tracks with pine needles. After climbing further all he had seen were the rocky walls, and could see no way of getting either through or over such terrain. He had gone back down and found a mountain stream rushing southwards, then looked for a spot to camp for the night, disappointed and frustrated, and angry with himself.

It had been during the morning when he was coming through the passage when he'd heard the command which came from above and behind him.

"Hold it right there, mister, and grab some sky." It had also been sheer luck finding the gap in the rock face. Early in the morning just before the light came he had heard stones rattling down the hillside through the deep timber, almost into his camp. After striking camp he'd searched and come upon the hoofmarks, faint in the pine needles but enough for him to see to track them till they ran back up to the bare rock which ran across the face of the mountainside. The man had to have come down from somewhere, perhaps from a pass, Mike had thought. A sudden rush of wind had drawn his attention to the rocky cliff and then to his amazement, he found the way in through a split. When he was on his way out of it, he had been stopped by the commanding voice; then another man, in his thirties, unkempt, wearing twin side-guns and holding a rifle pointed at his middle, had also barked out an order.

"Don't try going for your piece, or it'll be the last time you do."

Mike had sat still while the man came and took his Colt and rifle, looking keenly at him from light brown, bloodshot eyes. "What you doing up here?" he'd asked.

"I was hoping to join one of the gangs," Mike had spluttered out, rather hastily.

"Gangs, what gangs? What the hell you talking about?"

The man from above had come down off a ledge. "Better take him to Pick or Jordan. They'll see what he wants," he told the other man who nodded and took the reins and led the bay around a bend and out of the passage.

Jordan Coltrain, his brother Sean, and a man called Steve Pickings had questioned him for a considerable time. "How did you know where to find us? Who told you how to find the camp?"

He told them about hearing the rider come down and how he had traced the hoofmarks, then found the gap just by chance. They had exchanged angry glances, muttering something about Steel being careless. They'd told him he could bunk in the big cabin with the other men till they decided what to do about him. They had kept his guns.

He would never get out of this place. Coltrain had told him there was no chance, there was only one way in and out, and that all men were checked out.

He had told them his name was Mike Pollard. They went through his pockets but found nothing that mentioned his name. The bills of sale for Nero and the bay were tucked inside his hat band. They had searched his boots, even taken his socks off. They did not take his money, which was the only good thing.

At midday he had a meal with a lot of the men at a long table between the sleeping area and the cookhouse. No one said much to him and he made no effort to speak with them except to ask for the bread to be passed. Afterwards he went out and sat on a bench after buying some tobacco at the store, and rolled a cigarette.

"I seen that feller in the saloon in Holbrook," Tim told Jordan. "He might be an agent. He's been real smart to track us all this way."

"Ain't that smart: he'll not get out of here alive. His story don't hold water," Sean said scathingly.

"I'll have another talk with him. We don't want anybody joining us, in any case," Jordan told them.

Mike was still angry with himself as he sat smoking and thinking about his plight. He was a prisoner, unless he could find another way out. There was no way of getting up and over anywhere, as far as he could see. He would just have to play for time. Might be here for weeks. He had heard these men went elsewhere in winter.

A tall thin man who looked as if he'd been a rangeman by the way he walked, came over to sit beside him.

"Howdy, you're new here, I gather.

I'm Tex Boone," he said smiling in friendly fashion.

"Mike Pollard," Mike responded guardedly. He wasn't sure why he had used a false name, except if he was forced to go out on a raid to prove himself, and got caught, then he didn't want his real name on a warrant, should it by some chance happen. "One hell of a place this. You move out when the snow comes, I heard," he said casually.

"Yep, some of us are going soon. Some of the men are going mustang-hunting till around October. A few go to Mexico, some to another hideout further south. You staying with us?"

"Can't say. It's not exactly up to me."

"Yeah, well, you gotta be suspicious of a fella comes riding in as you done. Can't figure how you found us."

"Was pure luck. I meant no harm, was fed up with my own company, that was all."

"You might try asking Pickings if you can ride with his lot. Me, I mostly go

119

solo. I done a few stagecoaches and one or two stores. But I'm riding with a few this time, going south, maybe to Mexico for the winter. I got me a few bucks as'll see me through till springtime."

Mike felt Boone had been sent to do a little probing. He was wary. "I've done a bank job back in the Panhandle; my partner got shot. Was in a train hold-up near Santa Fe. Small stuff, mostly."

"The horse you ride, he looks range trained."

"Yep, bought him off a rancher, some trail bum stole mine when I was sleeping in a dry wash, a couple of weeks ago. I've done cowpunching, a cowpony is best for rough country, as I see it."

"Yeah, I know. Anyway, you watch out for Pickings; he has a dozen or so men who ride with him, all hard cases. Jordan Coltrain and his brothers, they're hard. And Warris, he rides with 'em. He's mean, a killer. Seems like they lost their brother Pete on their last raid on a bank. Was a youngster. I did hear he was only their half-brother. Some say he's a 'breed. One of old Batt Coltrain's. He was a real hard case, but was good at planning things, then he got hisself shot in a brawl. Probably was drunk or I couldn't see anybody taking him. They sure got a good haul on the last raid, so Warris was telling everybody. Best not to get in a poker game with that lot," Boone warned Mike.

"I'm obliged," Morris told him. "Am I allowed to ride along the meadows? Is there another way out?" he asked Boone.

"Not as I know of, and I've looked, just in case. Best you be real friendly; don't get their backs up," Boone said quickly and got up and left when he saw Jordan Coltrain emerge from his cabin and set off across in their direction.

Mike changed his mind about Boone. He was probably just a petty robber, a bit out of his depth with these hardcase men. He could see how difficult it was, simply to ride out of this place without a plausible reason. These outlaws would be suspicious of any lone rider who might, in their estimation, be a lawman, a bounty-hunter, or, a Pinkerton agent who had managed to penetrate their forces.

Coltrain came and sat down at his side. "You'd better come up with some good answers about what you been doing and how you know about us. You put yourself in a bad spot riding in here like you done. If you don't check out you'll never get out of here alive." Jordan spat tobacco juice into the ground.

"A posse told me about you lot raiding a bank somewhere back in New Mexico. They came on me when I was camping. I guess they thought I was in with you. Was near the Arizona border," Mike lied, about the location. "I heard you and your brother Sean talking near Holbrook. So I thought I might like to join you. Like I already said, I've done small stuff. I'd like to do bigger things. An' I was looking for my horse; he was stolen one night while I was asleep. I reckoned it must be one of your men, not your brothers, someone else. I liked that horse real well; I had to buy another one, and that made me mad."

"I bet you're a damned bounty-hunter! We hang bounty-hunters when we catch 'em!" Jordan said angrily.

"Wouldn't have come in here if I was! I didn't go to the law in Holbrook when I could've. That ought to tell you something. I got no time for lawmen. A sheriff hanged an uncle of mine a long time ago. Said he was a horse-thief, and he wasn't. No sir, I got no time for lawmen!" Mike snarled, hoping he was convincing Coltrain.

Coltrain sat pondering. The man seemed genuine, but then you never can tell. "Well, for now you can stay. We have a store over there where you can buy what you want. You can make yourself useful chopping wood and such. We might let you go mustang-hunting, only if you go out, there'll be someone with you at all times. I got no need for anyone else in my gang, and Pickings ain't looking, so we'll decide about you in a few days." He got up and walked off in a long swinging stride. A blonde woman was waiting for him at the cabin, he took hold of her and they went inside, and Mike heard them laughing.

The plateau was lengthy, the cabins about half-way along it. Mike went to saddle the bay; he might as well get acquainted with the surroundings, it looked as if he would be here for some time. At least he wasn't tied up. How long would it be before Pete turned up, and what was likely to happen when and if he did, he wondered rather apprehensively. As Uncle Henry used to say, "Well, Mikey, we're sure in the cowpats again".

"I sure as hell am, Uncle Henry!" Mike said plaintively.

8

JUST below the snowline, Pete Coltrain was lying amongst some rocks. He was dressed in the new clothing he'd stolen and glad of the thick jacket. It had taken an hour to climb to his eyrie after leaving Nero tied in a ravine under thick dark pine. He was opposite the cabins about five hundred yards higher, and had a clear view of movement and activity along the plateau. The sky was clouded which he was glad of and had he gone higher he would've been into thick mist. He could see several men cutting timber and chopping logs, and he focused the spyglass that José had lent him, which he used to find straying sheep, upon the Coltrain cabin. After Batt had been killed, Jordan had told Pete to move out into the main bunkhouse, and brought his woman in. The more he thought of how he'd been treated, Pete became determined they would pay for it. Suddenly a man went to the corral and stood patting a horse. "Mike, it's him," he uttered. What is he doing in there? He must be an outlaw! Disappointment rushed through Pete. He could hardly believe his eyes. Now he'll've told them I'm alive. Of all the stinking luck! Why in hell did he save me? For what reason? Maybe he didn't know who I was, but he knew about Jordan and Sean. Thought there was something about him. Too secretive!

Pete shrugged. Why did it matter? They didn't know where he was, nor when he would show up. What if he's a lawman, or an agent? Well, he'll never get out of there alive. If he is, Jordan will soon have him shot. If I could get him out, but if it snows much more, it won't be easy. How did Mike get in? He must've known about the hideout, must've had friends in there. The more Pete thought about it, the more he wondered. He would have to think some more about a plan.

Morris went over to the store and bought more papers and cigarette tobacco, then set about making a few smokes to put in a tin. Later he ran into Jordan when he came across to speak to a red bearded man called Buffalo Borden. When he'd finished talking Mike went to ask him about leaving. "I hadn't planned on being cooped up for weeks. I thought maybe you'd be going out on another job. I don't have too much of the ready."

"You can mark up in a book if you run out of dough, then when you go on a job, it comes out of your cut; only there's nobody going out as wants you, so you'd better pay for what you get, and do some hunting for food when Buffalo goes; he'll lend you a rifle. You can't get out unless I say so."

Mike spluttered. "I hadn't figured on being cut off."

"That's your misfortune then. We might be going after mustangs soon, I'll decide if you can go. Meantime,

there's poker games, and woodcutting."
Coltrain turned and walked away
leaving Mike angry, his face red. They
still had his guns. Maybe the best thing
was to try and tie in with Boone and
those who were leaving soon. It seemed
his only chance, and he didn't want to
leave his guns behind.

For the next few days he took the
bay along to graze and helped cut logs
for the big fire in the bunkhouse. The
more he studied the slopes the more
hopeless his situation looked. More
snow came on the peaks and Mike
had to buy a heavy wool jacket. His
sheepskin one he'd used in Montana
had fallen off from behind the saddle
somewhere back in New Mexico, and
he had not wished to ride back perhaps
twenty miles or more in search of it. If
he was thrifty, he need not spend too
much. Buffalo always came with him
when he went hunting for game. They
had stolen his guns; but then that was
what they were, thieves. He felt sure
he would never get them back. He was

virtually a prisoner, and it was his own stupid fault. Now he would never find Nero, not unless that boy came riding in here, and he was beginning to think that something must have happened to him. He hadn't felt so upset since Uncle Henry got killed, well not quite that bad, but bad enough. He hummed as he rode the bay across towards the small lake at the far end of the plateau, the horse turned its head and gave him a look. Mike smiled briefly.

He had been in the camp more than a week when one morning he got up shivering and found there were no logs beside the hearth. A grey damp mist went straight to his bones when he went out to collect an armful of logs. The horses were moving about restlessly, nickering and some were snorting. He went back inside, dropped the logs and walked along to Boone's bunk. "Tex, wake up. I think there's a cat or maybe a bear at the horses. I have no gun. You better hurry."

Tex grunted, some men growled.

Mike shook Tex again.

"What the hell, take my rifle: it's under the bunk. I ain't moving; it's too damned cold," Tex grunted.

Mike found the rifle, then he put on his heavy jacket and went out closing the door softly. He strode over to the corral where some forty horses were still nipping and biting, at the far corner. He went along the rails trying to see if there were any pad marks. When he got to the corner he stood quite still, staring, his mouth agape. The sorrel horse gave a half squeal, half nicker and Mike rushed up and got through the rails. "Nero, you old son of a gun! I'll be doggone!"

Burying his face in the horse's mane, Mike put an arm up over the animal's neck. He couldn't believe it. For some moments he and Nero stood close while the other horses went back to their slumbering. So, he was here. Where was Pete? Had he made it up with his brothers? Why else would he have come inside? Perhaps he'd had second thoughts about killing his brothers. He had no one else. What would he tell them about him? If I could just take Nero and ride out now. They'd cut me down faster than I could blink. Maybe they're waiting for the chance. The bay came snuffling in then and almost got into a fight with Nero. Mike slipped away quickly and got back to his bed. He lay thinking hard, in a turmoil. Somehow he had to get away and take Nero with him. If Pete hadn't made it up with his brothers, he must be somewhere around. He won't know I'm here. If his brothers left him to die that day, it had to be for a reason. Pete won't forgive them for that. I wouldn't have, if it had been me.

Mike was almost asleep when the door opened and three men came clattering in. One of them struck a match and went searching for empty bunks. After some cursing and grumbling from men who'd been awakened, the three threw themselves on to bunks and soon snoring floated down from the far end. Mike tossed and turned, then he got up and dressed himself and went to the cookhouse and made some coffee.

When the mist had lifted, the sun hit the plateau with the heat of Indian summer. Everyone was outside. Some were just sitting, others mending gear or getting ready to cut wood, or hunt game for the pot. The horses were let out to graze along the plateau.

Jordan Coltrain sat in a chair on his porch, the blonde woman stood behind him trimming his hair.

Mike had taken Nero out of the corral and saddled him up when Warris came looking for the roan. He was nowhere to be seen, and after mounting one of the mules he had gone to check amongst the loose horses. He came back and hauled in the mule in front of Jordan. "Jord, my horse, the roan, he's missing, he's gone!" he spluttered hysterically.

"What do you mean, he's gone?

Can't get out of here — the lookouts would have seen him. Wouldn't run off on his own, anyway."

"I've looked everywhere. I seen that Pollard and Boone they's going after bighorns, and Pollard, he got a good looking sorrel. Says its his, the one was stolen from him."

Sean and Tim came out on to the porch. "He's acting high-handed. How come a horse shows up like that and the roan disappears? Anyway, Jim, the roan is for Tim. Pa paid a lot of money for that horse, so it stays in the family. You can take one of the spares, or get a mustang when we go after some."

Warris stood muttering, his eyes rolling; he had been drinking heavily since coming back to camp. He dare not get into a confrontation with the Coltrains. Fuming inside he went off to go find one of the spare horses. He was sick of the Coltrains. Nevertheless, he was puzzled about the roan. It was unlikely it had got out through the night. It had been in the corral.

Maybe Sean was playing one of his stupid pranks. He could be real mean and spiteful at times. He caught up one of the spare horses and put his saddle on it, then taking his rifle he whacked it into a lope and went along the plateau. The big meadow was about two square miles, not counting the slopes. He passed one of Pickings' men, told him he was going to try and bag a deer, or maybe a sheep.

The creek that ran through the meadow formed a small lake at the far end, then it ran on and descended a dip into a ravine and went through a tunnel under a wide expanse of rock. When it rained or thawed the creek rose and the tunnel filled almost to the roof. At present the water was low and when Warris had gone past the lake, he went on beyond some elder bushes and tied the horse out of sight. He built a cigarette while he raked the open land towards the camp to check if anyone followed him. Five minutes later he was pushing his way through thick bush at the creek edge just before it disappeared. He stepped into the water and waded forward bending as he entered the tunnel. A short way in he was able to straighten up and step on to a ledge of rock about two feet wide. It got darker as he went further, then he came to a cave about twenty feet wide where he struck a match and found the lamp hanging from a wooden peg stuck in a crack of the wall. If Sean had brought the roan in here, it was a cruel joke. There was no sign of the horse. The cave extended another hundred feet, and then the water dropped out from a ledge down into a pool about fifty feet below. A horse could be got out under the fall and along a ledge, then up a steep slope. It was only possible when the water was low. It was also possible to come in that way. No one other than the Coltrains knew of this escape route, as far as they were aware. It had never been used, but Batt Coltrain had usually kept the lamp there just in case, and had told Warris he would kill him if he ever spoke of it to any of the others, particularly the Pickings men.

He was about to blow the lamp out and hang it back on its peg when a sound at the far end caused him to turn and look back. He was sure there was someone standing in the light of the exit, just a dark silhouette. He felt a sudden chill, then a voice called to him. "Warris, you took my horse! Left me to die! I will kill you for that!" Then there was a horrible laugh that faded away.

Warris stood rooted, frozen into immobility. He could not see a face, but he knew the voice. He blinked, then forcing his arm up he rubbed his eyes. Slowly he brought up the rifle, but there was no one there. All he could see was the light at the end of the tunnel. He whirled and stumbled, the lamp fell from his hand. Then another horrible laugh echoed through after him. Into the water he went, slithering and sliding till he got to the bushes, crawled up on to the bank and lay there panting.

For a while he just lay quiet, then he got up, untied the horse and mounted and set off into a gallup back down the plateau.

Sweat poured from his face as Warris arrived back in front of the Coltrain cabin. Jordan and Sean still sat drinking coffee and looked up in surprise as Warris slid to a halt. "Jord, Sean, gimmee some whiskey! I just seen Pete's ghost!" He got down and sat on the porch step shaking uncontrollably, jabbering incoherently.

Sean ran inside and brought a whiskey bottle and gave it to Warris. "He's got the screaming meanies, for Christ's sake! Been hitting the bottle too hard, lately."

"No I ain't! I tell you I saw him, right there in the tunnel! I went to see if you'd hid the roan in there. Kind of mean thing you do, Sean. Well, all I seen was a form then he said he was going to kill me, and gave a horrible laugh. Then afore I could shoot, he was gone."

Sean laughed. "Like I said, he's seeing things. First he lost Pete's horse, now he sez he seen him. You're losing your mind, Warris!"

Jordan Coltrain had known Warris for nigh on six years and never before had he seen him in such a state. Never seen him run scared. It was surely strange. "You go rest, Jim, and stay off the bottle. Tomorrow we're going after mustangs over to Black Rock," he said, and helped Warris up. He watched him as he took the horse and walked away muttering to himself. Thoughtfully, Jordan went inside.

9

AFTER putting the fear of God into Warris, Pete Coltrain climbed back up the slope from where he'd come out by the waterfall on the far side of the tunnel. He was chuckling but his thoughts were anything but humorous. He had not expected to see Warris in the cave. He had gone to fetch his bag of personal things, and the money which he had hidden in a crack in the roof of the cave where the water would not reach it. Apart from the $9,600 that had taken a long time to save, there was a silver medallion which had once belonged to his grandmother, and the only thing he had from his mother. The medallion was from the Mimbre tribe, and he had worn it around his neck until he'd been brought to live with the Coltrains. He had a certain pride in it and often wondered about his ancestry. To survive here though, he must be as American as possible. He knew he was part Spanish, part Indian, on his mother's side, and part Irish and English on his father's. No wonder, he thought, I am sometimes confused. He wondered from which part his desire to kill those who had left him to die, came from. There were also some wooden carvings he had made himself and two fine silver bracelets. Maybe one day when he met a girl he liked, he would give them to her. He would buy land and settle, somewhere over to the south-west, when he had finished what he had to do.

When he returned riding a different horse, José Garcia made no comment, but he saw the horse was, in fact, the roan he had ridden before. He helped Pete dig a hole in the floor of his shack and watched the boy place the bag in it then cover it over. Then they lifted the table over it. Pete had extracted some of the money and put $250 in the lining of his right boot, and gave $50 to José. "I will be staying around for a while, this is for food when you go down to Flagstaff. If I should not come back, you take the bag with you when you move. Keep it for one year, and if I have still not come back, then it is yours," he told the Mexican, whom he trusted.

Garcia nodded. "*Si, comprende*," he said then went to get on with his chores.

* * *

Jordan Coltrain came across to Mike who was busy cleaning out the hoofs of the two horses. "How come you claimed that sorrel?" He asked rather stridently.

"Because he is mine. I rode him all the way down from Montana, then he was stolen one night while I slept in a drywash some weeks ago when I was in New Mexico. Some men rode in here last night, I reckon they were the ones who stole him."

"Then you better call 'em out," Coltrain said snidely. "Cash Dexter and his boys ain't likely to take kindly to you calling 'em horse thieves."

"I've got no guns, and they've already said they know nothing about the horse, so I'll let it go. I've got Nero back, that's all that matters."

"I haven't time to discuss it now. I came to tell you you can go with us mustang-hunting. We need all the help we can get. If you try running for it, you'll be shot."

Mike remained tight lipped; he'd like to put his fist into Jordan Coltrain's face, but the time wasn't right. He went to get the bay and Nero ready, so he could use them both, and mostly to make sure Nero stayed where he could see him. The weather remained bright and cold at night, the ground frosty in the mornings. He actually enjoyed the chasing and was ready to drop at the end of each day. At the end of two weeks there were 800 mustangs penned up ready to be broken. Most of the time he had kept company with Buffalo Borden and Jim Warris. Borden, a big red-headed man nearing sixty was affable and Mike enjoyed his company. Warris was morose and jumpy and kept watching the timber and skylines, as though expecting someone.

"You think the Coltrains will give me my guns back soon?" Mike asked of Borden as they rode along a ridgeback.

"Can't tell with Jordan. They think you could be a lawman. I'd be careful if I was you. You'll have to prove yourself before they'll trust you. You put yourself in a bad spot coming in the way you done."

"If I was a lawman, I'd never have come in," Mike replied bitterly, still feeling cross with himself. He was glad though that no one had challenged him over Nero. He had given any of the men who'd remarked on the horse, cold chilling looks which had made them back off. To them he was an unknown quantity, a man without a gun, but how well could he use one should he get one in his hand?

A gang of men worked almost around the clock to break the mustangs, a hard and dangerous task. Some horses broke legs, one or two got away, some were retained. Then some older men who no longer took to the outlaw trail, drove the horses to the Flagstaff railhead for the army.

The horses, some of them scarred up, made between $15 and $25, and all told brought an amount of more than $15,000. The men who'd done the breaking got the largest cut, and Mike was pleasantly surprised to find he got $350 for his part. He had managed to put a lariat on a very good-looking black stallion which Pickings badly wanted. He felt satisfied. He had not expected to make such a sum of money for ten days' work, and he had possibly put Steve Pickings in a more affable mood.

"Why'd you let Pickings have that

stallion?" Warris asked Mike as they sat in the bunkhouse eating a huge meal of steak and potatoes, having cleaned themselves up after the days of toil.

"A stallion is nothing, only a nuisance. I prefer a good gelding. I expect Pickings thinks it makes him more of a man to have such a horse," Mike said scathingly. "I only let him think I was keen on it, so's he'd give me more."

"Pick is a mean devil — best not get on his wrong side. He could have taken it from you, so I guess you were right."

"I'm not looking for trouble, Warris. You seemed out of sorts today," Mike changed the subject.

"I thought I seen a rider up on a ridge, like he was watching us — had a roan horse, did you see him?"

"Nope, I was too busy." Truth was, he had seen someone though the sun had been in his eyes and the rider was gone when he got a clear view up the ridge. "You're getting spooky, Warris. You ought to lay off the bottle."

Mike had heard about Warris's odd behaviour and noticed the Coltrains had played it down, which was hardly surprising since they'd said Pete was dead and they had buried him out in the plains of New Mexico. The whole thing had set Mike thinking. If Pete had got Nero in and his own horse out, there must be another way in. It was also probable the Coltrains knew of it, but no one else seemed to believe there was another way in or out. Boone had said he'd looked and found nothing.

Warris went off after the meal and sat on his bunk with a bottle of whiskey.

"He'll not last the winter if he keeps it up," Buffalo Borden reckoned. Buffalo had turned to robbing when he'd run out of money, and got sick of trapping and hunting. He was fast with a side-gun, but his eyes were poor for rifle work, and he had to wear his steel-rimmed spectacles to read the out-dated magazines and papers that lay around the bunkhouse. He was good natured, however, and Mike enjoyed his long discourses on the wilder days when he was young. Though he thought it was hardly peaceable when men went into banks killing folks, and robbing stages and such.

Warris went to find Jordan. "I tell you I seen the roan up on the ridge today when we was on our way back. I'm sure that Pollard saw something, only he ain't saying nothing. Maybe it's a pal of his, the law mayhap."

"Warris, you're becoming loco. If you don't lay off the booze you'll go plumb out of your mind," Jordan told him.

"We got no time here for jabbering idiots. Maybe you'd best ride on if you're scared. Boone and Larry Cord and those heading south are leaving anytime soon," Sean said.

"Jord and me, we've been riding together a long time. I tell you I saw Pete in that tunnel. It was his voice."

"Listen, Jim, tomorrow we'll go take a look around. You go get some sleep.

We're all tired after the mustang hunt."

"I reckon Jim has a conscience about Pete. Never thought to see it in him," Sean said as they watched Warris walk away, his head lowered. "Supposing he's right though?"

"What you mean, Sean?" Timothy interjected. "You all said Pete was dead. How in hell can it be him?"

"Well, Pete's horse disappeared. Now that Pollard is riding another horse he says is his. None of the boys know how it got in here, and it wasn't one as been left up in the timber when they rounded up the spares. It's a good horse, and range trained. I don't feel easy about Pollard. The story about Steel going down was a lie, I'd say. I think someone told him where we are at, and I got an idea maybe it was Sam Steel; he never mixed much."

"Oh, knock it off boys, we'll go take a look tomorrow, or we'll all be spooked next," Jordan said angrily.

The day was dull and cold, a hint of snow in the air and thick low clouds hung over the slopes. The Coltrains got saddled up, and with Warris they left, taking rifles and side-guns with them, and rode along the plateau.

"Might as well get us a bighorn or two," Tim said excitedly. Hunting game was a thing he enjoyed. Secretly he wished he owned a big ranch, down in one of the long valleys where he could ride about freely and get himself a wife. Since Pete was gone he missed him. Jordan and Sean were close being older, and often left him out of things, but if trouble came they'd stick together, that he was sure of.

Warris took a track that went up the west side as the others split and went further along. He pulled up and took a hip flask from his pocket and took a long swig of whiskey. He felt the chill in his bones. Jord believes me about the kid, I seen it in his face. The kid wasn't dead. God knows how he survived and got hisself here. What if it is the whiskey? Naw, it's him:

the horse has gone. He thought a lot of the roan, his pa gave him. Wish Batt was here now. Warris went on, thinking hard and muttering to himself. When he'd gone up almost out of the timber he came to a halt; he could see very little, the heavy mist had come down again after clearing for a while. He pulled the horse in as it snorted, startled as if it had heard something. Warris sat still and a sound came to his ears. Sounds carried in the mist and became weird and distorted. The track led past a rocky outcrop and Warris got down, leaving the horse by the rocks; he took his rifle. Must be a sheep, he thought. "I'll prove to them Coltrains I ain't loco, by God! A bit of sheep meat will make a change!" Stealthily, he went forward.

The mist thinned again and Warris saw he had strayed on to a ledge and stopped quickly. Again he thought he heard a noise and started to back up slowly. The noise sounded like something scraping against the rockface. He levered the rifle and stood very still.

"Warris, I'm here! Can you see me? No use shooting a dead man! I'm dead, remember? You all said so!" The voice came out of the mist.

Warris let out a strangled shriek as the mist blew about in swirls. He fired wildly. His hands shook so much he couldn't lever the rifle again.

"You can't shoot a ghost, Warris!" the voice floated to him from behind and then the terrible laugh.

Warris let out another shriek, turned, letting the rifle drop. As he turned his foot slipped, and his hands tried to clutch at the towering rockface, then he pitched out into space, letting out a terrible scream. His body fell downwards striking the tops of the blue pine, then slid off and bounced into some jagged boulders, and lay there.

Pete Coltrain gave a chilling laugh, then he retreated upwards into the mist, climbing between rocks till he hit a tiny sheep track and went across the slope and worked his way down to the creek where it was thick with bushes, then went into the water and disappeared inside the tunnel.

When he got to his horse he mounted and rode on down as the sun broke through on the other side of the mountain. He told himself he had not killed Warris, it was an accident. He spooked and fell, that was all. Well, that was one down and three more to go. It wasn't going to be easy.

When the rifle shot came to Jordan's ears, he looked up to his left. Jim must've found a bighorn, he thought. He turned and rode towards the slope where he had last seen Warris heading upwards. There was a clattering of hoofs below and he saw Timothy coming up fast.

"I heard a scream, Jord," he yelled as he came up.

"I heard a shot. Maybe Jim's seen a bighorn."

"It might have been a cat, we'd best go see. The scream was awful.

I don't like it, Jord." Tim pushed his horse on.

They traversed the slope back and forth making their way upwards. They could see fresh hoofprints on a game track and followed them carefully in the thickened mist. A horse nickered, then Warris's horse came slithering down to them. Timothy got down and grabbed the reins before the horse trod on them and went hurtling downwards.

"I don't like it," Jordan said. "He might've run into a cat, though it's a bit high for cats. The horse didn't run, neither."

Swinging down, a nasty feeling in the pit of his stomach, Jordan went forward checking the ground, taking advantage of the mist suddenly clearing a little. He saw the ledge and halted, and he also saw some heelmarks. "The fool must've gone on the ledge. Jeez, he must've fell off!"

"Maybe he saw another ghost," Tim said laughing.

Jordan swung round, his eyes blazing.

"You say you heard a scream. You see how the mist comes and goes. Let's get down below and check."

"Look, here's his rifle," Tim went past Jordan and picked the rifle up, his face grim.

They got back on their horses, and leading Warris's went downward into the timber. "Where the hell is Sean?" Jordan looked about worriedly.

They came upon Warris's body lower down in the rocks where it had landed. When Jordan got off to look, he could see that Warris was broken up, both his arms and probably his back, he thought. The eyes were open and had a look of sheer terror, as though he'd had a shock of some kind.

Sean came up to them then and slid off his horse. "I heard some shots. What's going on?" Then he saw Warris. "God Almighty, what happened to him?" he gasped.

"Must've fell off the ledge under the rock up there. Maybe he went after a sheep in the mist, silly devil!" Tim said, his face pale. He felt scared all of a sudden.

Jordan's eyes met Sean's. Timothy saw the look that passed between them. "You think he's alive, don't you? There's no such thing as ghosts. It was Pete up there! It was him took his horse back! He's going to kill all of us! You left him to die; you said he was dead!" he shouted.

"Shut up, Tim! Just you shut up!" Sean shouted back.

Jordan turned the body over to check for bullet holes. He found none. He asked Tim for Warris's rifle, and sniffed at it. "Been fired," he said. "He shot at something, an' I don't believe it was bighorn. They'd not go on the ledge, it goes nowhere, and they ain't stupid."

"You think maybe he was thrown off?" Sean looked keenly at Jordan.

"We never saw any other boot marks. If there was anyone up there, how could he have known where Warris was headed?"

"Pete never knew about the tunnel,

not as I remember. Pa said nobody but us and Warris should know about it," Sean said worriedly. "Maybe one of the men followed. They know Jim had plenty of dough."

"Come on, put Warris on his horse." Jordan told his brothers. "We'll find out where everybody was this morning, especially that Pollard."

"I think we've all got spooked," Sean said as he found the broken bottle in Warris's pocket, and laughed. "Next thing *we'll* be seeing ghosts." He laughed again. The others said nothing, the laugh was a hollow one.

10

WHEN the Coltrains rode in with Warris's body draped across his saddle, men came pushing forward looking askance at one another.

"Damned fool fell off a ledge up on the west slope, was after a bighorn sheep. Never should have gone up that far in the mist," Jordan told the staring men.

"Maybe somebody pushed him off," Sean blurted out. He saw Pickings looking angry. "We want everybody, to say where they've been since breakfast."

Pickings stepped forward. "Why would anybody want to push Warris off the ledge?" he asked suspiciously.

"For his poke, I reckon."

"You saying you really think he was pushed? Is that what you think, Jordan?"

"It had occurred to us," Jordan answered. "Warris knew this place well, and he was usually careful. Only he has been drinking a lot lately."

"That's right," Buffalo Borden added his voice. "Had a lot on his mind, been doing a lot of shouting in his sleep." He gave a significant look towards Jordan.

Jordan knew Buffalo had given him a warning. Borden was no fool. "We'll bury him proper tomorrow. He was my friend. He made me his beneficiary. He had nobody, and he writ it down and he said Buffalo was to have his rifle if anything was to happen to him." Jordan looked around at the men, a defiant look on his face.

The men shuffled and there was a lot of muttering as they dispersed.

Boone had witnessed the bringing in of Warris. "I'm riding out tomorrow with a few of the others," he told Mike as they stood near the corral. You going to ask if you'll be allowed to ride with us?"

"No, I'm sticking around a while in case they go after more mustangs. I have an idea I might settle somewhere around here and get me a job. If I had more money I could get me a piece of land. I'm tired of this life."

"Then you'd best go further north of the big canyon, I hear there's lots of mustangs up that way in Utah. You'll break your back and maybe catch only a few, and you need plenty of help to break 'em. Ain't hardly worth it!" Boone said, shaking his head.

Although he'd used the idea as an excuse for sticking around, Mike thought it wasn't a bad one at that. He had to stay to find out about Pete. He was sure it was he who'd had something to do with Warris's falling, or *had* he been pushed? Maybe he'd been frightened off the ledge. He had heard the scream while he was at the lake. It was a quiet beautiful spot, and he liked to take the horses there to graze. He figured if he bided his time, didn't get their backs up, the Coltrains might just let him ride out. It had also occurred to him that they may have been responsible for pushing Warris off the ledge: it was they who were to gain from it, and they had all ridden off together. There was no one in the camp, however, who would dare make anything of it, not even Pickings, whom he could see wasn't entirely convinced about the Coltrains' story. Mike also found out later that the Coltrains were trying to suggest that he might have had something to do with it. Since he had seen no sign of Pete, it occurred to him it might have been the Coltrains who'd put the idea to Warris that Pete was around somewhere. Perhaps one of those three men *had* brought Nero in. Might have come across Pete on the trail or even found Nero somewhere. It seemed plausible. Maybe he should just try to get away and ride on.

A man called Preacher read from a Bible over Warris the next morning. Mike did not attend the funeral, it was all he could do to keep from laughing about the hypocrisy of it all. He was sure no one cared a damn, least of all the Coltrains: they could hardly wait to get the whiskey out after it was over. Warris was laid to rest behind the cabins, just near the trees where there were a half dozen or so other graves, mostly neglected, and the wooden crosses blown down.

There was a good deal of whispering in the bunkhouse that evening, and Jordan had produced the letter that was supposedly written by Warris. "Never knew he could write," Mike heard one man declare. It was usual when one of the outlaws got killed, and had no kin, for his money and other items to be dispersed amongst the men. Even Sean and Tim had been suspicious of the letter Peg Muldair had composed and which she claimed Warris had given her to keep. She'd even stamped on it to make it look as though written some considerable time ago.

Buffalo Borden was pleased about the rifle. He and Warris had known each other longest. He said nothing about what ran through his mind as he sat carving Warris's name on a piece of stripped pine pole, for a cross. Warris hadn't been a good sort of man, but he didn't like it if there had been treachery in his death.

Mike was sorry when Boone and several men rode out before first light. He was ready, however, when Jordan sought him out as he sat smoking, watching Buffalo groom his horse.

"I thought you was eager to ride out, Pollard? You and Boone seemed friendly."

"You still have my guns, and I figured if you were ready to let me ride you'd have given them back to me," Mike replied with considerable acerbity of tone.

"Ah yes, well you never came and asked me. You can have them. Pick and all of us agreed. You can go. Only not in daylight, you know that. Tonight when it goes dark. It feels like rain or more snow. We'll all be leaving soon.

So you come and collect your guns before you leave."

Mike hadn't been prepared for this. He smelled a trap. He hadn't missed the conference earlier between Coltrain and Steve Pickings. He had also seen three men ride out some time after Boone and his group left.

"I was thinking about mustangs," Mike stalled. "I'd like to have another go at them. Maybe stick around till spring, they'll be coming down lower now."

"You want to hunt mustangs, you go find your own; we don't want no poaching on our terrain, and we don't want you with us. You don't drink hardly worth a damn, and you don't play poker nor womanize. And where the hell were you the other morning when we went hunting with Warris?"

Mike bristled; if he wasn't trapped here in these mountains, and had his gun on, he'd have called Coltrain.

"I was fishing up at the lake," Mike said evenly and saw, from the corner

163

of his eye, Buffalo edging away.

"An' you never heard nothing?"

"I thought I heard a cat yeowing. I heard a shot. Then later I saw you coming down off the slope. I figured it wasn't my business."

"All right, tonight you go. I'll tell the guard to let you pass out the gap."

"If that's the way you want it. I'll be taking both my horses. I need one for packing; I'll be taking a few things with me."

"You take the horse you came in on. Leave the sorrel. You got no proof it's yours."

Mike went red. "I'll take the sorrel, leave the bay. I let Pickings have that stallion. That seems fair enough to me."

"The sorrel is the best horse. You leave him. If you ain't satisfied then you can walk out for all I care." Coltrain swung away.

Unable to think of what else he could do, Mike was furious. "I'll go in the morning before light," he flung at Coltrain who was really getting up his nostrils.

Coltrain stopped a moment considering, then he swung round. "Yes, that's OK. See you do! We never invited you to come here!"

It was a bitterly cold wind and it cut into Mike's face as he rode Nero along the plateau. He couldn't even collect his guns till this evening. Supposing he rode out and tried to sneak back in again on foot? Go and get Nero and slip out again while the guards were inside the small hut they used at night. They'd be cold, and wouldn't figure on anyone else coming or going after he'd gone out.

No, it wouldn't do, they might have someone following him. He couldn't trust them. He would have to watch his back all the way to Flagstaff. Jordan agreed to the morning because otherwise I'd have been suspicious. If he has sent men out, they'll be waiting out there somewhere. Looking back he could see two riders coming along the edge of the opposite side of the plateau. He put Nero into a lope and rode almost to the lake then pulled in and got down. He left Nero to graze while he sat on a deadfall tree and had a smoke and kept an eye on the two riders.

Mike sat for almost a half hour. His mind was in a turmoil over Nero. He could not ride away and leave him. He might have to shoot his way out. They'd probably shoot Nero out of spite. He saw the two riders go further along so he called to Nero and went into the timber. He was into the saddle quickly and moving upwards. He headed for the spot he felt sure Warris had been, just under the wall of rock that was lost in the mist. He thought about Warris; if he had been thrown off, it would have to be by someone who could get close enough to him. Someone who knew him, not a stranger, nor a ghost, albeit that of Pete Coltrain. From him he would have backed away in fright. Maybe that was what had happened. Warris had seemed all right that morning at breakfast. The mist was chilly and Mike made to turn back. Then Nero pricked his ears and made a soft nicker. Mike thought he heard something and sat still trying to peer through the mist. A soft rain had started to fall. He felt his hair stand up on the back of his neck as a form appeared before him, then a voice said, almost in a whisper, making him jump out of his skin; *"Amigo! Como esta?"*

Nero nickered again and put his muzzle out to Pete Coltrain as he came to the top side of him, so that he would not be seen from below.

"Pete, you almost scared me out of my wits! What in hell are you doing up here?" Mike said rather crossly.

Pete grinned, and patted the horse. He had on his thick clothes and a rabbit skin hat with flaps over his ears.

"I see you get your horse back, *Señor* Mike. You see I took good care of him for you. He is a very nice *caballo*," Pete said smiling widely.

"You little bastard, you left me in that desert. I had to walk miles and carry all my gear." Mike looked angry but inside he was pleased to see the lad.

Pete's face went dark. "So, now I'm the half-breed *bastardo*! All the time I think we are *amigos*. You saved my life. Now I see you ride with my brothers. The ones who leave me to die," he said bitterly.

"Listen, Pete Coltrain! I don't ride with your brothers by choice. I followed them because I knew you would come. I found them in Holbrook when I waited for you. Even heard them discussing you. Then I was sure who they were. I even saw the vet who stitched you up. It was the only way I figured to get Nero back. Did you kill Warris?" Mike threw at Pete quickly.

"He kill himself, he fell from the ledge!"

"Don't come all that Mexican pigeon

talk with me. You speak American well enough, same as I do, amigo!"

Pete grinned, and Mike looked anxiously down the slope.

"What do you intend doing now?" Mike asked Pete.

"I will kill my brothers then I will ride to the south then west. I will buy some land for myself."

"You are a fool to go after them. You will have no chance, you'll only end up at the end of a rope. Is it worth that just for vengeance?"

Pete ignored Mike's question. "Why don't you ride, now you have Nero?"

"They wouldn't let me. I have to go in the morning before light. They want to keep Nero. I don't know what to do. If I ride out on the bay, I'm sure they have men posted to snipe me. I'm sure they think I'm a lawman or an agent. I found my way in by accident, and went riding in there, like a fool. I've been thinking of a way out of my predicament."

"I will take Nero out for you. Then

you ride down in the thick timber. They will have men out there, for sure. If I had known you were in there I would not have taken Nero in. I meant to take him later. I took my own horse and left Nero, because I heard some men coming and had to leave him."

"I don't want you to take any risks for me. You got your life back, keep it. You're young, enjoy life; don't throw it away, *amigo*!"

"Tonight, I will take Nero. You go back now. I see you later. The men, they come across the valley," Pete turned and walked off into the mist.

When Mike reached the bottom, the two men who rode with Pickings' gang met him as he came out of the timber, assuming surprise. "Oh, it's you Pollard! You ought to be careful going up there in the mist. Could have a nasty accident, same as Warris," one of them said chuckling.

"Thought I saw a deer. Could've chased it down for you," Mike said smiling. He felt he owed these two no explanation but he wanted no trouble now. "It's a nice place here; I'd like to have seen it in springtime. I'm leaving in the morning. Be heading for Tucson, more than likely. Might pick up a bit of spending money on the way." He winked at the two of them disarmingly.

Dunstan said, "Yeah, they say you're a loner. You make much that way?"

"Sometimes folks on stages carry quite a lot in their wallets, and women wear jewellery. I don't care for robbing banks much, a partner got gunned down when we tried it. It's easier to get away in some lonely spot on the trail."

Ledbetter nodded. "You got a point there. There's always a big posse after a bank raid, and big rewards; just puts bounty-hunters on your trail. Look what happened to the kid."

"What kid?" Mike asked looking puzzled.

"Pete Coltrain. A posse shot him.

Jordan had to bury him real quick some place in a desert. So he said."

"Too bad," Mike said and pushed his horse past the two men before he might say something he'd regret.

★ ★ ★

By the time Jake Chandler had ridden across to the ridge where he saw the rider, he found no sign of him. And after casting about for some time it got too dark so he made camp in a deep hollow not far from a creek. It was three days later that he came to the conclusion that he'd perhaps ridden too far north. He had lost all sign of fresh hoofmarks, though there were plenty of unshod marks left by wild mustangs. He decided to turn round and set off back again, disgruntled, knowing how Procter must have felt when he'd tried to pin down these outlaws. By late afternoon a storm hit him with an icy blast forcing him to seek shelter in an old cabin once belonging to trappers.

He spent the night and after breakfast he rode out again heading into a long valley and from the bottom of a ridge he saw horses streaming along the valley floor. There were many riders urging the mustangs forward, no doubt into a trap they had set some place. He pulled his glasses and focused on the riders. He drew in his breath and put his attention on a big red horse, and a dun. The dun had no distinct markings, its back looked honed in the sunlight. It was the one, he was sure. The man riding it, the same. Though they were a long way off, and he could see no faces, he was sure it was the same man who wore a plaid jacket. Then on the far side of the mustangs, he saw the big bay, the tall man atop of it. By God, as if they hadn't enough money from the robberies! Now they were chasing mustangs, and probably passing themselves off as legitimate wranglers. Nobody would bother to investigate them. Nobody would have seen their faces. They robbed in other states and came back here to hide. Maybe they bought up cattle with the dough, and maybe they had a big ranch some place. What could one sheriff and a deputy do about it, Chandler wondered. Anyone found snooping too closely would more than likely get a bullet. Never be heard of again.

The strung-out mass of fleeing mustangs was gone from sight, but Chandler now had a place to start looking. To find their hideout then bring in the posse, that was what he must do. He swung down off the horse to lean on a boulder, and as he turned he trod on a loose jagged stone; his ankle gave way and he went headlong, striking his head on a tree stump jutting up from the ground.

The dun had stood for quite some time. It became restless and paddled about. The sun had gone down, the air was quite chilled. Fretful, the horse backed and pulled and the reins slid from the bushes where he'd been tied.

Not seeing his master he whinnied and moved down sniffing the air. The dun had gone some forty yards when it came upon Chandler and thrust its muzzle down at his face.

When Chandler felt the rasping tongue lick down the side of his neck he stirred. He rolled on his side moaning. Then he reached for a clump of grass and pulled himself up. The horse nickered softly. "Doggone it hoss! What the hell happened to me?"

Putting a hand to his forehead, Jake felt a fair sized lump and some crusted blood. When he tried to get up he let out a yelp. "Busted me dog-blamed ankle," he snapped.

He got hold of the stirrup leather and hoisted himself to stand on the good leg. After a moment or two he managed to get into the saddle with difficulty. The best thing he could do right now was to go back to the cabin, it was a damned sight nearer than a two-day ride to town. He might just run into that bunch of outlaws, too, if he tried riding down that valley right now.

It was sundown by the time he reached the creek by the cabin, and let the horse drink. His canteen was full so he angled over to the cabin and got himself down on to a chopping block at the rear, then tied the horse up and hobbled round into the cabin. An old kerosene lamp he'd used the last time still had a little left in it so he got it lit, then sat down. Pulling his knife from his belt he slit the boot down and with a lot of sweating and cursing got it off. Thank God the leg wasn't broken. The ankle was badly swollen and extremely painful. Angry at himself for being so careless, Chandler pulled a bottle from his saddle-bag and drank about a cupful. Then he chewed on some beef jerky and lay on the bunk feeling sorry for himself. Later, he managed to hobble out again and brought in some logs that had been left at the side of the cabin, from some time back Chandler figured. He got a fire going in the stone fireplace and warmed himself and made coffee. Then he went to bed.

In the morning Chandler realized he was in no shape to ride, so he came to terms with the fact he would be stuck for two or three days till the swelling went down and he could at least use a moccasin on the foot, if he couldn't get the boot on and tie it with something. It was not the first time he'd been holed up in such a place. It was not such a calamity, except the outlaws might be gone by the time he got to town and got some help. He was sorely vexed.

In the cabin he found a spare bottle and after managing to scramble on to the horse, he went down to fill the canteen and the bottle. He let the horse drink, and after they got back he hobbled him behind the cabin so he could graze. The sun was out again and he sat in front of the cabin, his rifle over his knee in case a deer should come into his sights, or anything or anyone unwelcome.

For three days Jake Chandler stayed put, hobbling around to tend the horse and ride him to the creek for water. His food was almost gone, and he'd not seen anything to shoot. He must return to Flagstaff, he decided. There was nothing he could do the shape he was in, and it looked as if snow might be on the way, the peaks were constantly shrouded.

When he did finally make it back to town, with his boot tied up with string, the ankle still painful though the swelling had gone down, he was dejected and felt rather a fool when he arrived at the rooming-house. First he had a decent meal, then after sending Clara Nolan to get him a bottle of whiskey, he drank about half of it and passed out into oblivion.

The next morning, Sheriff Procter almost told Chandler "Well I did warn you," but refrained from doing so. Men like Jake Chandler he respected. To go in search of those hardened criminals was sheer folly on one's own. He sent the doctor round to look at the sprained ankle.

A week of Clara Nolan's cooking had Chandler back to good spirits again. He'd watched with Procter when some men brought the large number of mustangs down to the rail-head. He saw no one he recognised, nor any of the horses they rode. The men visited the saloons afterwards and when asked, they said they'd come from up the Kaibab. No one could dispute their claim. The men were middle-aged and it was possible they did not consort with the outlaws other than to bring down the mustangs and take back the money to them.

To take a posse up into those mountains on Chandler's information, a man who imbibed liberally, Procter thought, would be foolhardy. There was not enough to go on.

11

MIKE MORRIS sat thinking hard about how to get away from the camp when he became aware of Buffalo Borden sitting next to him, speaking in a whisper. "Sorry, Bull, I was thinking on what I'll do next when I get away."

"When you go, you be real careful, son. They got men out there waiting to kill you."

Mike smiled. "I guessed as much. Why're you siding me, Buff? They'll kill you if they find out."

"I don't always like what Steve and Jordan do. I got a feeling they killed that boy, and maybe Warris. They always blamed Pete for their mother leaving when Batt brought him here. Was a half-breed Mexican. I liked him. Now you watch out, mind your back. Go left out from the gap and straight

180

down into the thick timber. That way you'll have a good chance."

"I'm obliged, Buff. You take care, too," Mike told the elderly man whom he had grown to like. He finished his meal and packed his utensils with his gear, then he strode determinedly across to the Coltrain cabin and rapped soundly on the door. Sean opened it.

Mike said coldly. "I've come for my guns. I'll be on my way before sunup."

Sean yelled back into the room. "Jord, you want Pollard should have his guns?"

"Yeah, give 'em to him. Never know what he might meet!"

Mike heard the guffaws, and in a few minutes Sean brought the rifle and Colt. "I guess I must've used the shells," he said grinning as he handed the holster belt with its shell slots empty. The guns were also empty, Mike found as he turned and walked away without a word. He heard the door slam behind him. He hoped he would not have to see any of the three Coltrains again.

Back in the cabin he cleaned the guns which had not been used for some time. He felt, rather than saw, one of Pickings' men watching from his bunk where he lay. He filled the slot in the butt of the Winchester, and levered one into the breech. Then he put five shells into the cylinder of the Colt.

Borden brought him a coffee laced with whiskey, and Mike took it gratefully. After drinking it down he lay on his bunk smoking. It was only nine o'clock. The time dragged and he knew he would not sleep. He wondered if Pete was out there somewhere, and hoped he would do nothing rash. It occurred to him then that there *must* be another way in other than the gap, or how had Pete managed to get in and out without being spotted, especially with his horse, or with Nero, and out with the roan? It ain't worth getting himself killed, even for Nero, he thought.

The men made their trip outdoors

before settling down for the night. Two were missing but Mike knew they were visiting with the girls. Two more were at the lookout shack. He dozed till the warmth from the fire cooled, he could hear the men breathing heavily in sleep, one or two snored. When it finally got to about two o'clock, Mike got up and drew on his boots, then his thick jacket and taking his rifle, and saddle-bags he went to the door, opened it and slid out quietly, then closed it. He went quickly over to the corral to look for Nero. He called softly, but there was no answering nicker, then a soft muzzle poked through the rails. Mike felt relief, but then disappointment. He'd hoped Pete might have taken him. He had no way of knowing exactly what the lad had in mind. Of course if Nero had not been there he would not know whether Sean Coltrain had been the one to take him and hide him somewhere. Perhaps he was too early. He decided to go back and wait another hour. In misery he lay tossing on the bunk, his head splitting from wondering what he should do. Almost an hour went by then he decided. He would go, take Nero, and leave the bay.

Sean Coltrain had had a fair amount of whiskey when he left the large shack where the girls lived. It was frosty and he shivered as he relieved himself near the corral rail. A smile came to his face and he crossed over to the tack shed and picked up a halter. He went back to the corral and slipped in through the rails and searched for the sorrel. Nero backed off snorting at the man who smelled strongly of whiskey. Sean snapped the halter on to the head collar and led the horse out through the gate, then shut it. He took Nero round to the rear of the Coltrain cabin and tied him to a pole he used for breaking mustangs.

Sean sniggered. "That Pollard ain't getting you! Sneaky devil, he won't need you anyway after Cash puts a bullet in him." Nero snorted and

Coltrain left him and went round and entered the cabin. After pulling off his boots and outer clothing he slid under the blankets and was soon snoring loudly.

★ ★ ★

Pete Coltrain slid round the large boulders at the end of the narrow gap into the hideout. He could hear the two men talking in the small hut used at night by the guards. They would have a bottle, and there was a stove for warmth and making coffee on. Making no sound in his boots covered in rabbit skins that left no prints, he pulled his revolver from its holster and in a few quick steps was at the door. He thrust it open and rapped out an order. "Put your hands up quickly where I can see them. Don't make me have to say it again!"

Bob Mitchell let out a shriek and dropped the pipe from his mouth, lifting his hands slowly.

Doug McDonough gulped and put his mug down on a table. He lifted his hands quickly. Both men stared, their eyes never leaving Pete Coltrain's face as he advanced, keeping his gun on them. He lifted their side-guns, then he took the rifles that were standing against the wall and shucked the shells, then threw the rifles outside.

Neither man made a move to stop him. Saliva dropped from the corner of Mitchell's mouth.

McDonough said, "Holy shit! He ain't dead! Poor Warris. Nobody would listen to him. He thought you was a ghost."

Pete laughed. "I am a ghost!" He tossed a rope to Mitchell. "Tie him up and hurry, or I'll lay you both out." He shoved the revolver into Mitchell's back.

"One shot and you'll have the men down fast."

Pete grinned nastily. "I don't need a bullet, I have my knife; it is very quick, you'll feel nothing."

Mitchell blanched. "Do as he says," he said hysterically.

After Mitchell was tied up, Pete made McDonough lie on the floor while he tied him hand and foot. Then he blew out the lamp and left, closing the door behind him. He ran swiftly up the grass going round the rear of the cabins when he got to them, almost a mile from the way out. He saw Nero tied behind the Coltrain cabin and went to him as the horse snorted then put his muzzle into Pete's hand. So, Sean had taken him, now Mike would not know he was here. He untied the horse and took him to some bushes close to the graves, and tied him to an overhanging branch. Next, he went to the storeroom and found a small drum of kerosene which he put outside. The store had never been locked. Any one who was found stealing was hanged. Pete remembered the rule grimly. Batt Coltrain had personally invoked the rule on a man who'd broken it, and hanged him from a tree.

Since the bay was in the corral, he knew Mike was still in the bunkhouse so he settled down in the storeroom to wait. For a young man he had a lot of patience. He believed it was inherited from his Indian ancestors. Inside he was calm. Soon it would be done. It would be over, *acabado!*

★ ★ ★

Mike, once again got up from the bunk, and took the blanket with him and went out feeling the coldness. He went to the lean-to where the saddles were stacked and picked up his own and a bag with his gear. There were still about twenty horses in the corral, the mules were kept in a smaller one. He couldn't find Nero anywhere and cursed. He should have stayed outside and watched; then he would have been frozen to the bone. He couldn't waste any more time so he went to the bay and put the bridle on him and led him out, then got him saddled. The horse took the saddle willingly and was ready to be on the move again. Where the hell was Pete? Has he taken Nero? How far will I get before a bullet comes out of the night? The moon was too bright now. Another hour and it would be the false dawn. Mike put a foot into the stirrup, then he heard a sound over by the store.

"*Amigo!*" he heard the voice whisper and put his foot back to the ground. As Pete came over to him, he whispered anxiously, "Nero, he's gone!"

"Don't worry, I have him. I found him back of my loving brothers' cabin," Pete said bitterly. "Mike, the guards are tied up. You must go now. You take Nero, I will bring the bay. Give me ten minutes then I let the horses out. I'll run them down through the gap."

"Pete, come on now! Leave it be! I have plans to catch mustangs come springtime. We could go cowpunching till then. We could be *amigos*," Mike said earnestly.

"They are waiting out there to kill you. If I send the horses out it will throw them off guard. It will take all day searching to round them up. Go straight down through the timber; after you cross the creek the other side of the first ridge and over the log bridge, go left along the creek. Do not follow the trail. A mile or so on you will come to a ravine. My horse is there. You wait for me. But don't wait till it is daylight. If I don't come, take my horse and go to Flagstaff. I will find you there. Don't argue! Go now!" Pete said and helped to put the saddle on to Nero. Then Mike rode off, feeling strained and exposed as he rode for the gap, expecting a bullet to thump into him any minute.

Pete tied the bay and waited until he thought ten minutes had gone by. He was thinking about Mike: he wondered if he would see him again. Catch wild mustangs he'd said. Go away together, work on a ranch till spring.

He asked me, Pete Coltrain, the half-breed bastard of Batt Coltrain who nobody gave a damn about, 'cept José. *Amigos*, he said we could be *amigos*! Quickly he opened the corral gate and got behind some of the horses and flipped a rope at them, got them moving gingerly towards the open gate, then a large black that had been caught when they were chasing the mustangs put its head up and sniffed and then broke into a run. Pete got it going in the direction of the gap, the others followed, one or two milled around till he moved them on. He hoped no one would hear them sniffing and sneezing as they put their muzzles to the frosted grass. The black was running with at least ten horses behind him. He smelled freedom and was soon at the gap and running through, the others going more cautiously.

After one last effort, Pete left them and ran back to get the kerosene. Again he worked quickly and poured the kerosene around the front porch of the Coltrain cabin and round the side. Then he struck a match on his boot and threw it on to the porch, and ran like hell for the bay. He did not stop to find a saddle, as he could ride well enough without one, and gathered up the rope bridle.

The flames spread rapidly, crackling and sparking as Pete sat watching from within the trees behind the cabin. Then came shouting and yelling from inside the cabin, glass breaking, and a form came falling out through the side window. One by one the Coltrains came out, Sean, throwing a bundle out before him, Tim, then Peg Muldair and last of all, Jordan, cursing as he rolled on the grass to put out flames attacking his long johns.

Men came pouring out from the big bunkhouse, shouting, running on bare feet, and in various underwear.

Pete could hear Sean almost screaming with rage. "It must've been that bastard, Pollard! He took that horse as well! I'll kill him!"

"The boys will get him," Jordan shouted as Pickings came up with a gang of his men to try and put the fire out. The creek was too far away and what water there was in the barrels was soon gone. They were too late. The cabin caved in as bullets exploded inside from the boxes the Coltrains had not had time to rescue.

It was then that Pete came riding fast, his six-shooter in one hand, the rifle and rope bridle in the other. He fired close to Jordan, making him leap back and almost knock Pickings off his feet. Pete emptied the revolver and went racing past them. None of the men had a gun with them. He swung round when he got past them. "I'll haunt you Coltrains, as long as I live! You left me to die! I'll haunt you, you scum!" With that he turned the bay and sunk his heels into him and was gone fast down to the gap.

"Get him, somebody!" Sean screamed at the gaping men who stood rooted, forgetting the coldness, unable to believe their eyes.

Buff Borden stood at the back of the circle of men. He suddenly let out a loud guffaw, then turned and went back to the bunkhouse. He got a bottle out of his bag and sat laughing till tears ran down his cheeks. He'd never seen anything so damned funny. The Coltrains out there in their long johns, Peg Muldair in her nightie all shivering and cussing; the shack burned down, and young Pete, he done it. Mike has gone, and I bet he makes it clear to Flagstaff. Then he sobered a little as he realized all the horses were gone including his own, and the mules had kicked clean out of their corral and were gone right along the plateau braying like billy-oh. "Ain't nothing I can do till daylight," Buff laughed, then he put the bottle to his lips and took a long long swig. "Sure glad that boy ain't dead! Them lying sons-o'bitches said they buried him. Well he sure enough got up out of that grave, just like Warris said he done. Steve Pickings won't never trust Jordan again."

Jordan Coltrain came storming into the cabin shivering and cursing, his long johns all scorched black at the rear.

"By God! I'll kill that 'breed! I'll kill that damned sneaking little bastard!" he barked as he stood with his back to the fire.

"Thought you done that already. Warris said you buried him back in the desert," Buff said scathingly.

"Aw, shut up Buff, and give me that bottle!"

Sean and Tim came in then with some of the men. "All that money gone up in smoke! All that goddamned work for nothing! I'll string the little bastard from the nearest tree when I catch up with him." Sean snarled.

12

THE three men who waited in their separate places had lit fires to keep warm while they waited within hearing of the trails Mike Pollard was most likely to take. They had not been well pleased when a rider had come to tell them Pollard would not be coming till just before dawn. They'd been offered a hundred dollars each by Pickings and the Coltrains to do the job. Not all the outlaws were in funds; some had lost at poker, and a few had been unlucky of late. It meant nothing to them to pick off Pollard.

One of the men, Jack Ford, was dozing by his low fire when he heard a horse coming crashing through the timber. He threw the blanket off his shoulders and jumped up. His own horse whinnied and then a dark shape came running to it. He could see the horse was riderless and had only a head collar on it. "What the hell!" Ford muttered and went to catch up the horse he recognized as one from the corral. "How in hell did you get out?" he said and tied the horse alongside his own.

About to return to his fire, he stopped to listen as more snorting and movement in the trees came to his ears. "By God, somebody must've left the gate open," Ford said, puzzled as more forms came moving down past his camp. He tried to get a hold on one of the horses, but it took off in fright and the others followed. Ford pondered for a while then decided he best go back to camp and see what was going on. Up above the trees towards the rockface he could see a sort of glow in the sky. It came to him as he got cinched up and mounted, after throwing earth on the fire, that maybe Pollard had started something. He could have let the horses out.

★ ★ ★

When Pete Coltrain went out through the gap, he went down over rocky slab and into darkness of thick timber. He could hear horses way down below moving in the underbrush. Very carefully, but with some urgency, he headed over a ridge and then down to the creek where the bay stepped nervously going over the tree bole bridge. Pete stopped now and then to listen, then went on following the creek and didn't go on up the trail, as he'd instructed Mike not to do. It took a good half-hour to get through thick undergrowth and over rocky and rooted ground in the darkness. The moon was gone and the timber made it dark. When he got to the ravine he listened a moment or two then called: "*Amigo*!"

Mike heard the call with great relief. "Up here!" and Pete soon came up to him. He winced when Mike thumped him on the back, joyously. "I was worried for you."

Pete grinned. "That hurts, take it easy."

"Sorry, I forgot," Mike apologized. "You stink of kerosene, what on earth . . . "

"Come, we'd best get going." Pete ignored Mike, cutting him off. He led his own horse, after tying the bay behind it to the tail, and Mike followed wondering worriedly what had gone on back there in the camp. He was too well hidden in the ravine and thick timber to have seen the glow in the sky, which by now was almost gone.

For more than an hour they led their horses stumbling over roots and rock, going around bushes and threading in and out of trees, staying as close as they could to the creek. The light was coming up in the east when they came at last to grassland.

Mike stood scanning the valley, his breath making vapour clouds. A sleeve of his jacket had been torn and he felt dog tired and looked at his scratched up boots giving a brief smile. "I'm glad we're out of there," he told the lad, whom he knew was no longer a boy but a grown man with a lot of turmoil and bitterness inside him. He knew just how he was feeling; he'd gone through it himself; he knew how it was, and it hurt.

"I think you are safe now; nobody comes that way. I know these mountains, I had plenty of time when my father and the others all rode off and left me, before they said I was old enough to ride with them."

"What happened up there? I thought I heard shooting," Mike asked. Had the boy somehow managed to get at his brothers and kill them? he wondered anxiously.

"I set their cabin on fire, after I let the horses out." Pete turned and grinned, but his eyes were hard, contemptuous, and they returned to searching the terrain, and Mike could see he was all tensed up.

It's the Indian in him, Mike thought.

"You mean you set fire to the bunkhouse?" He looked aghast.

"No, only the cabin where my brothers slept and the woman. Jordan's woman!"

"My God! Did they, did they get out?" Mike looked in horror at Pete.

Pete sat chuckling. "Oh yes, they got out. They came out the window yelling and shouting. Jordan had his rear on fire, and he rolled in the grass, but he wasn't hurt. I came out of the trees, riding fast. I shot off my gun and the men who were all there in their underwear, were trying to put the fire out. I shouted at my brothers, 'I'll haunt you for ever', then I rode off, and they stood like they'd seen a ghost. It was wonderful! They looked so angry, and they were cursing and Sean was yelling, 'that Pollard, he must have done it'. I wish you could have seen them. Now they've gotta spend all day looking for their horses, and we'll be gone."

Mike laughed with relief. "I'm glad

you didn't kill them, even though they deserved it. Now you can ride away without having it on your conscience. Let's get to town; I need a bath, and a damned good drink, and then some sleep. I need that most of all!"

Pete turned to Mike then. "I can't go with you, not yet. I have something I must do for a friend."

"You're not going back up there? They'll kill you if they see you! Forget 'em, they're not worth it!"

"I'm not going back there, only to another valley where an old friend has his flocks and I promised to help him move them. You wait for me in Flagstaff; Jordan and the men, they won't go in there. I don't forget you saved my life. When I come, we will have a drink together. Maybe we get drunk . . . "

"OK *amigo*, I like the idea. You take care!" Mike swung up on to Nero and set off at a lope along the side of the valley, heading south. He had gone quite a way when he realized he'd forgotten to bring the bay along. Well, I'm not going back, he thought, he could see no sign of Pete. He began to wonder if that was the last he would ever see of him. *Quien sabe?*

★ ★ ★

After the initial shock had worn off, the Coltrains had raided the store and found some outer garments to wear. Fortunately they had managed to throw out their boots and Jordan had saved his rifle, though the butt had been scorched, and he'd had to search for it in the grass where he'd thrown it and forgotten it till later.

"I bet Pollard had something to do with it. I can't help but think he was somehow tied in with Pete." Sean opined later, as they sat drinking coffee before the daylight came. "I guess that sorrel really was belonging to Pollard, way he was riding it and the horse knew his name all right. Queer kind of name that, Nero."

"What makes me so goddamned mad," Jordan said furiously, "is all that money just gone up in flames! All that planning and time wasted! Don't give a damn about the cabin, we ain't coming back here, anyway. Oh by God, he'll hang all right when we catch up with him!"

Timothy said little as he listened to his brothers. He had thought Pete to be dead; they'd said so, Warris and his brothers. Steve Pickings came in looking peeved, and he too spat out what Timothy was thinking, "Thought you said you buried that kid, Jordan!" He was furious; he had to waste hours looking for his horse and that stallion would never be found now. It had torn itself loose from the lean-to where it had been tethered, and gone. He'd paid Pollard good money to let him have it.

"We hadn't time to stop," Jordan spluttered. "We had a posse on our tail, and was no use us all getting caught to save one of us, especially that damned half-breed pa never should have brought here in the first place."

Pickings gave him a hard look. He would probably have done the same if it had been he who'd been there with the Coltrains. He was angry, nevertheless. He didn't wish to have a posse coming up the valleys before they got away.

"We'd better share out what's in the kitty now." He turned to Jordan. "Soon as I get my horse, I'm on my way. I reckon this place is finished now, and there's nobody left to look after things."

"Yeah, well I'll go fetch the tin." Jordan got up and went to the store to fetch the money tin which held the payments for what the men had bought. Normally it would be used to bring in more supplies for next spring, but now the hideout seemed no longer safe, everyone agreed the money should be shared out, and whatever was left in the store would also be shared.

Jordan picked up the money box

from under a counter. He quickly took a batch of notes and shoved them into his shirt pocket, then went back to the bunkhouse. There was just over $800 and some loose coins.

"Don't seem much! All that liquor and clothing, smokes and food and all!" Pickings grumbled, looking at Jordan.

"Some of the boys who left, I gave 'em a share-out. You saying it ain't all there?" Jordan reached for the Colt he had taken from the store.

"Just seems light, that's all!" Pickings daren't push his luck with Coltrain.

The eighteen men left shared the money amongst them and took whatever was left of provisions. No one wanted the mules, but Jordan said they would be used, two of them anyway, to pack the girls' things, and Buff could then have them. The other four, he claimed himself. He said his father had bought them in the first place.

It took most of the day to find their horses, and everyone was in a foul mood afterwards. Pickings and his men rode out just after dark, mumbling something about maybe they would see Jordan and his brothers in Tuscon.

Sean had been ready to pull a gun on one of the men who'd made snide comments about the Coltrains and their lousy 'breed brother who'd spoilt the hideout for them. Peg Muldair had stepped between them. "I'd not be saying anything about trust, if I was you boys. I reckon there isn't one of you who wouldn't sell out, if you thought there was plenty of dough in it. I guess I've had enough of hiding away. Me and the girls are heading for Denver. There wasn't any damned thing to do here all day, and you lot weren't over-generous. Worst summer I ever had!"

Jordan raised his head sharply. "You needn't look at me for any financial pay-out. All my dough went up in that fire. Now we'll have to make another hit somewhere just when we was planning on lying up for the winter and having us some fun." Jordan was bitter because Peg had confided she had hidden *her* money in a bag at the bottom of the flour barrel in the store, and he knew she had a fair sized bankroll.

In the morning Jordan got the girls started after pulling a wagon out from a hiding place down in the timber. Buff Borden and the cook, a man almost as old as Buff, rode along by the wagon which Peg Muldair elected to drive, using the two mules to pull it, since there were no spare horses.

The three Coltrains and a man called Crauchuck waved them off, then they sat smoking, well hidden within the trees while they thought out where they would go.

"I'm for finding that kid, first," Sean said savagely.

"Thought we might swing on down to Prescott," Jordan said. "I wasn't going to let the others know where we was heading. Best we ride, can't stay hanging around here. We can make camp later and think things out proper," he added.

"We owe Pete for what he done to us. Near on $70,000 we lost in that fire, and our belongings. Lucky there was things left in the store."

"Jeez, as much as that!" Crauchuck looked with respect at the Coltrains. Maybe he was right to tie in with them.

"Between us, yeah! We got what Warris had, as well. If we could just make us another hit like that last one. How much you got, Dean?"

"About $500. I lost over a thousand to Pickings and I spent a bundle in one or two places, and on the girls. I'm for making another hit. What about the train, you thought of that?" Crauchuck looked at Jordan.

"Trains ain't easy," Jordan informed Crauchuck. "When they got money in a safe, they got them newfangled locks on 'em. Takes too long, and they got guards."

"There's a long stretch after Williams.

We could just throw the safe out, and let the mules pull it away, then blow it open, if we had some dynamite," Crauchuck suggested.

Sean got excited. "We should have kept Buff with us, he always carries dynamite."

"Buff's too old now, and I didn't like the way he was friendly with that Pollard." Jordan shook his head. "Could get on as passengers and lift the wallets off the other passengers. I ain't keen on it though. Often get lawmen travelling on trains, and agents.

"We can't be sure Pickings isn't heading for Prescott. I know Buff is. Maybe we should go to Phoenix."

"Why don't we hit Flagstaff then go to Phoenix? If we're leaving this area, it won't matter. We never done it, and we know the layout. Cash told me all about it when he was thinking about doing it. They got a side door off an alley," Tim interjected.

Jordan looked brighter. "Well, if we do it, we gotta be sure the girls have left. Don't want any trouble there, and Peg would maybe see us and wave or something."

"We don't owe her nothing; she soon gone off you, Jord, when you lost all your dough."

"Shut up, Sean! I know well enough you was making it with her behind my back. Was tired of her, anyway!"

Crauchuck looked sideways at Sean and saw the colour creep up his neck. Lucky he was Jordan's brother or he'd sure as hell've been dead by now. Maybe they did kill Warris. Maybe he shouldn't get involved with the Coltrains.

By the time the late fall sky had put on its hues of incomparable beauty, the Coltrains were ensconced in a hollow screened by aspens, close to a creek. Far behind them rose a high mountain peak, and closer in lay dark masses of timber. They soon had a fire going, and sliced up deer meat sizzling in a pan, the last tins of beans heating on the fire. The sky changed into the blue-black of evening and stars began to show as a soft wind soughed through the trees. Somewhere south of them a train whistle hung in the air. The horses, tied to a line strung between the trees dozed quietly alongside the mules.

After they had eaten Jordan passed a bottle round. "If you're riding with us, Dean, you better know I'm boss. What I say goes. We've done real good so far. Warris took too much on hisself. He killed the manager in Socorro, and that put the posse on our trail fast. Mind you, we don't want you if you's scared to do what has to be done. If you get my drift?"

Crauchuck dragged on his stogey. "I never been shy of doing what I have to do. There's one thing though, I expect them as I ride with to back me up, if need be."

"Fair enough," Jordan replied. He lay in his blanket thinking about Peg. For three years she had been with him, and seen the camp got supplied with girls. Now she was gone. Just like that. Damn it he missed her, but he had been thinking of dumping her, after he found out about Sean and her. "Damn you Sean," he said. "Next time you shack up with my woman, I'll kill you! You hear me?"

Sean lay looking up at the stars, wishing he was in a saloon somewhere, or in a cat-house. "Sure, Jord, I hear you." He smiled and closed his eyes. Jord must think he was still in knee pants, just like pa used to.

13

AFTER three days of waiting, Mike Morris had seen no sign of Pete. He was bored with hanging around, and annoyed about his other horse. He was also worried in case Pete had fallen foul of the Coltrain brothers. He was staying at the cheapest hotel he could find, trying to preserve his limited cash which was rather higher than before he'd gone mustang-hunting. That was the only good thing to come out of his enforced stay with the outlaws. The blacksmith had told him it would be unwise to travel all the way on his own to California, especially to try crossing either Death Valley or the Mojave Desert unless he had a guide. On consideration, he thought it would save Nero a whole heap of hard travelling, he'd already had a long hard journey. It would be best to take the train. If that youngster don't show by tomorrow I'll be on my way, he thought somewhat sadly and disappointed. He hated leaving though without knowing if Pete was all right.

The subject of Mike's thoughts was, in fact, several miles south of Flagstaff. He had helped José Garcia move his flock, travelling hurriedly, letting Garcia ride the bay, using his burro for his pack, and with two dogs they had managed to get the sheep and goats to some land where a few Mexicans lived and where there was a spare adobe.

At first light, after a few hours' sleep, Pete said his farewell to his old friend and rode north again, a feeling of excitement within him, as he pondered on the new life he was about to embark upon. Mike was like an older brother, one he could respect and have love for, not like those Coltrains who had never wanted him. I'll change my name, too, he thought.

As Pete Coltrain rode north, his brothers were moving west of Flagstaff, intent on their plan to rob the bank there.

A couple of miles north of them, Jake Chandler, having lost sight of the roan horse and rider, had spent the night tucked in behind some boulders. He had woken up suddenly when he heard shots, then seen the glow in the sky. He'd packed up quickly and ridden off a ridge east of the route up to the outlaw camp. He heard the horses and pushed his dun down through the trees, and seen a flicker of light from a camp fire. He knew something was going on and it had to be the outlaws. They must be moving camp. When he got down to where he'd seen the light, he found the spot where a fire had been doused. He kept in the timber till daylight, and then he saw men rounding up horses, and he could only guess as to what had taken place. His patience rewarded, he had managed to trail the Coltrains.

After spending the night in a drywash, out of the wind and where he could build a low fire and cook the rabbit he had speared at a run with a sharpened piece of wood, so he did not have to shoot it and alert the men, he had eaten it ravenously, and then slept. He had been up before the Coltrains left their camp and ready to keep track of them. The big bay left imprints Chandler was now familiar with, the horse had a long stride. He had seen the red horse, a dun and a black. The roan was no longer with the foursome, and the man on the black, he'd not seen before. What a prize if he could just get the drop on them. He was prepared to put a bullet into all of them in a leg or someplace that would make it easy for him. He preferred having them alive, so they could go for trial. If they were all dead when he took them in, it would only be his word that they were the bank robbers from Socorro, and it might look bad. It was unlikely he would get the chance to kill all four, anyway, Chandler thought.

When they swung west and then

circled south-east, he became suspicious. It looked as though they were heading for Flagstaff. When they halted a few miles north of the railroad tracks, Jake figured they might be thinking of hitting the train. They made camp under some cottonwoods near a creek. By morning it was drizzling and overcast.

The men did not hurry to move out. By the time they were packed and on the move again it was almost nine o'clock. Looks as if they are heading for town, Jake reckoned and put his field glasses away. He smothered his fire and got mounted. After considering a while, he lit out and cut across to go down behind a shelf of land and used it to cover his progress. After about two miles he slowed up and stopped near a gap in the bank. He could see the riders still heading east now, and loping steadily.

Jake was almost in sight of Flagstaff when he rode up on to a bluff and sat under some cedars. The riders were well behind him and were halted under some trees. Some time later they set off again, and this time they had left the mules behind. Now what could that mean, Jake wondered? Either they're going in for provisions, or, could it be they were going to hit the bank? Whatever it was, it didn't matter, 'cos they were *the outlaws* he and the posse had followed, and they had to be taken. He sunk his heels into the dun and rode fast for town.

Procter looked up from behind his desk in surprise as Chandler made his hasty entrance.

"They're coming!" he gasped, out of breath. "Four of 'em! They left some mules tied aways out of town, maybe three miles. Might be they intend hitting the bank just as it opens!"

"You're sure it's them?" Procter got up quickly.

"I'm sure; three of 'em, anyway; there's a new one."

"We'd best be ready. See what they do first." Procter went to unlock the rifles in the wall rack. He took down a shotgun and loaded it. Then he checked his side-gun. "I'll go warn Havers at the bank, and get some help. You go tell my deputy, he's at the livery, then go warn Hank Bailey at the big store. Tell him to have his shotgun ready. I hope to God you're right about these men! We don't want to kill innocent rangemen, or someone coming in on business," Procter said, looking stern.

"It's them, the big fella on the tall bay horse, and the other two, they were the ones we chased from Socorro. I know their horses. Don't know what happened to the roan!"

His face set hard, Chandler left the office and went to inform the deputy of what was about to occur. Then he went to the big store. Just as he was about to go in his eyes lit on the sorrel coming up the street from the east end. It had one white sock, and a white blaze. His mind clicked. That man, the first night. He had a horse just like that. Thought all along he was part of that gang. Seemed odd he was there at that time. He watched the man tie the sorrel in front of the assayer's office and then walk off to head down a side street.

Jake rushed inside to warn Bailey. A customer paid her bill and left in haste, and Bailey reached under the counter for his shotgun. Chandler went to stand in the doorway and stood gazing up the street, he was sweating inside his buckskin jacket. Maybe they weren't coming into town, maybe they were going to the railroad. They wouldn't have left the mules if they were taking a train. Was too early to come in to visit a saloon. It had to be the bank, Jake felt sure. An' all that money they got in Socorro, how greedy could they get?

Procter came walking up the other side of the street which had suddenly gone quiet. He went to stand in the doorway of a boot shop. The drizzle was heavier now. The bank would be open in five minutes; Procter consulted his timepiece. Only two reasons they were coming in early, and that would be to do some shopping, or maybe go to the blacksmith's. Outlaws only came to the saloons after dark, unless they figured nobody would recognize them. He glanced to the west and saw two hats appear where the trail came up from a dip. Then two riders, one riding a deep red, the other a black. He tensed and made a sign to Chandler who was also tensed, but ready.

* * *

Pete Coltrain rode easy; he had given Garcia the bay. He would pay Mike for the horse, but if he didn't agree, then he would have to go back for him. He put the roan into a lope, the horse slipping on the wet track. It would be good to leave this area and go to a new life. No more being told what to do! No more robbing and hiding! He wanted to walk down a street feeling free as most people did. Not have to hide from lawmen or bounty-hunters. He came to the Flagstaff trail and turned east. He could see the railroad track north or him. A mile or so further on he went down a steep slope and eased the horse into a walk. The trail was winding and as he came round a bend he saw two horses going up over the crest. He let out a gasp, sucked in his breath. It was Sean, and a man on a black horse. For a moment he wondered if he was mistaken and he looked back over his shoulder to see if anyone followed. To be trapped between his brothers would be the end for him. He pulled off the track and rode through some trees. If they were going into town, Mike could be in danger. As he came up out of the dip, he caught sight of the big bay and the dun. "*Madre de dios!*" he lapsed into Mexican. Mike was smart, if he saw them he would get out of town. Jordan wouldn't risk a showdown either, it would draw attention to him, and he wouldn't want that.

Pete remembered the sawmill at the

south side of town and headed for it. He tied his horse to some bushes near a flat car waiting to be loaded with lumber, then taking his rifle walked quickly towards the east end of town and came up a side street. Unfortunately, he did not see Morris disappear off the main street and head down towards the railway station.

Pete was wearing the poncho and a black Mexican sombrero that he had worn two days ago when he had stopped to buy supplies at the store for Garcia. He could not be sure someone might not recognize him from some past raid in another town. People moved about, especially Pinkerton agents; his father had warned him about them many times. He headed for the barber's shop across the street, pausing on the sidewalk as he observed two horses come down the street from the west and pull in across from the bank. He also saw, with a shock, Nero standing hitched further along at the assayers. He saw Sean swing down and look back, as though at the sorrel. He'd certainly recognize it, that was sure. Pete felt tensed beyond anything he'd ever felt. Sean would be wondering if Mike would see them, perhaps spoil their chances of robbing the bank, as Pete could see that was what they intended. He noted the saddle-bags over Sean's arm, and he recognized the other man as Crauchuck, a man Sean sometimes drank with.

Pete suddenly realized the street was not very busy. In fact there was an unusual lack of pedestrians and movement in the street. Then it was early. He looked down to the sheriffs office and saw two horses hitched at the rail. Up the street, he thought he saw someone in a shop doorway. He had a distinct feeling something was wrong. Had he been with his brothers holding the horses he would have been ready to call to them, not to go on with it. Where had Jordan and Tim gone to? Pete wondered as he saw Sean and Crauchuck go into the bank. He worried about Mike and then he went back across the street, not wishing to be caught on the main street if the Coltrains came boiling out of the bank and saw him. Out of spite they would try to involve him, he was sure.

Jordan and Tim Coltrain turned their horses into the alley that ran into the back street. They swung down and Jordan, taking his saddle-bags, strode to the side door of the bank and knocked, leaving Tim to mind the horses. He knocked again, then heard footsteps inside and then the door swung inwards. "I've brought a fairly large deposit from the Purple Canyon ranch. I'm the new foreman and Mr Dunstan sent me in as he's not feeling well. Thought it best to come to the side door," Jordan explained.

The man nodded. "You'd better come in," he said and stood aside motioning Jordan to enter.

Jordan saw the suit of a bank clerk, but he caught the distinct smell of horse on the man. He stepped forward feeling the man's nervousness as he coughed loudly. He also heard the hammer click back and swung round slamming the saddle-bags hard against the other's gun hand. The gun went off into the floor. Jordan pulled his own revolver and hit the man hard over the head, he dropped to the floor. Then he went swiftly up a staircase as he heard footsteps coming from within the banking area. Two men raced out through the open door, and Jordan ran down and shut and locked it. He went quickly through to the bank where a man in a black broadcloth suit stood holding a Peacemaker Colt, somewhat shakily, pointed at Sean who stood with his hands up shoulder high.

"Did you get him, Alf?" the man asked without turning.

"Sure did," Jordan answered, and hit him over the head.

The man slumped to the floor, and Jordan plucked Sean's gun off a counter and tossed it to him, also scraped some notes out of a drawer.

Crauchuck, who lay on the floor, started moaning and got to his knees just as Jordan yanked Sean behind the front door when he heard feet running on the boardwalk. The door was flung open, then an arm holding a shotgun was thrust forward, and Jordan hit the wrists hard that held the gun, it went off into the counter and Procter fell backwards on to the boards.

Sean ran out firing at forms he saw coming down the street. Men scattered quickly running for cover. Jordan came out firing hurriedly. He had the Peacemaker with him and fired at a man who came from the alley; the man was lifted off his feet before he fell backwards, dead.

Crauchuck was on his feet, he yanked the knife from its sheath at his belt, threw it at Procter as he came back in. The knife hit Procter in the arm and he dropped the shotgun, and Crauchuck rushed past him out through the door.

Chandler had worked his way down

from doorway to doorway; as Sean and Jordan were firing from behind a wagon, he saw Crauchuck come out of the bank and hesitate then he leapt off the sidewalk. He lifted his rifle and blasted Crauchuck in the chest. He fired again and Crauchuck fell back, and lay dead.

When Tim Coltrain heard the first shot, he hit the saddle and waited. When the two men came out through the side door, he fired at them and they scattered for cover under some steps leading to a loft. Tim got the horses moving and still holding the bay's reins he went out of the alley into the back street, turned east and coming to the cross section he went quickly to the main street. He could hear men shouting and feet running, so he pulled up at the corner. Across the main street he glimpsed a Mexican duck and run down the opposite side street. He sunk his heels into the dun and took off to cross the main street. He saw Sean and Jordan firing from behind the water trough and yelled, then headed down the sloping side street.

Sean got across to the horses while Jordan covered him, and yanked the rifle out and fired at the first puff of gunsmoke he saw. Jordan came then and they both managed to get on to their horses then they reined them to follow Tim. Jordan had taken the black, but he knew Crauchuck was down, probably dead. His side-gun was empty and he reached for Crauchuck's rifle, then as the horse balked he dropped it on the ground, cursing in savage rage. He was still trying to figure why the men had been lying in wait for him in the bank. How could anyone have known their plans? It had to be that 'breed, he must have seen them.

Bullets were coming at them now from all directions. He couldn't see if Tim had got away; there was no sight of him. Sean had pulled up at the bottom of the street when two men appeared and started firing at him. He saw him lurch in the saddle. He whipped the black round and went back towards the main street. There again a man was waiting; he charged the black straight at him and felt a bullet rip into his leg. The man had to leap out of his way, and Jordan got the horse moving down to the east end of town.

Tim had let go of the bay and was heading east when a volley of shots came ripping over his head from near the livery-stable. He swung round, not knowing what to do next. Then he saw the lumber and headed towards the rows of stacked planks. Ahead of him he saw some flat cars and hoped to get round them and head for the open land. It was no use trying to help Sean and Jordan there was nothing he could do for them. They would have to help themselves, he thought desperately. He was scared out of his wits as he got round the flat cars. Then he saw the roan: Pete's horse. "It was him, he gave us away! The sneaking bastard! By God, where is he? I'll kill him!" he raged.

When Mike Morris heard the shooting, he was on his way back from the railway yard. He'd bought a ticket for himself and Nero. He would leave a note at the livery-stable for Pete, whom he felt sure would go there to enquire about him. He set off to run up the slope. His horse was in the main street. He felt alarmed now. Had Pete come to town, and had his brothers seen him? All kinds of things went through his mind as he ran. When he got to the corner he looked round it, carefully. Men were down near the bank. Bullets seemed to be cracking all over the place. He ran keeping close in to the doorways and got to Nero who was snorting and pulling to get free, as were other horses next to him. He got to him and quietened him down. From over the horse's back he could see a man go down as someone shot at him from behind a water trough.

Then someone got up and ran towards some horses. It was Sean Coltrain, he felt sure of it. Then came Jordan who leapt on to a black. Both of them were firing, then Jordan dropped something and they were gone round the corner and down a side street. The stupid blundering fools. They must have tried to hit the bank. Oh God, is Pete with them? Oh no, he wouldn't . . . Mike set off running again as men came out from doorways and ran down side streets; he followed, drawing his Colt.

Jake Chandler went for his horse, mounted and ran it down the main street turning right at the livery-barn. He heard a horse coming and pulled in behind a shed and got down. The black came running and Jake took a quick aim at the big man who was looking back over his shoulder, the bullet hit him in the side, and Jake fired again hitting the horse in the neck and it leapt sideways throwing Jordan out of the saddle, and he hit the ground hard. The reins hung in front of the horse and it stood rasping.

Just as Jake stepped forward to go to it, a bullet whanged over his head. He whirled, his ankle giving way and he fell cursing loudly. Had he not fallen the next bullet would have hit him in the chest.

Sean saw Jordan on the ground writhing. He tried to get to him, but bullets were coming at him from Chandler's side-gun. He felt a sharp pain in his leg, then another in his shoulder. He got the horse moving to try and head out of town, but another bullet plugged into his side and he yelled clutching at the horn, then he fell over it. The horse went back to join the black which was bleeding from its neck.

Chandler was up limping when three men came tearing across from the livery-stable, and stood holding their guns on the Coltrains, waiting for the sheriff coming at a run down the street, his coat sleeve all bloody.

Pete was moving along the side

of the sawmill shed when Tim came around the flatcar so he stopped and flattened against the wall. Then two men came running past him. They started firing at Tim who took a bullet and yelled, but he came on straight at the men, knocking one over then charging at the other who had to leap away and lost his rifle. Then Tim turned the horse his way, and Pete could see the desperate look in Tim's eyes, blood running down his neck. He stood rooted in a kind of fascination as the dun came towards him. He could not force himself to raise the rifle and fire.

Tim saw the Mexican standing by the shed wall. What if he took the poncho? He heard a sound and turned as one of the men levered his rifle, and Tim shot him with his Colt. Again he turned towards Pete who was about to run for some lumber piles, but his eyes were on Tim who suddenly saw their blueness and shouted at him, "You, you sold us out, you scum!" He lifted the Colt and aimed at Pete just as a gun barked and, before he could fire, a bullet took him right out of the saddle.

The man who'd been knocked down, came to stand over Tim Coltrain who lay gasping his last breath.

Pete walked over and took one last look at Tim. He spat on the ground, then he walked away before the men could get a close look at him. Inside he felt numb.

He was half-way up the side street when he saw Mike coming at a run. He gave a feeble grin.

"Pete, thank God you're all right! I thought you might have been caught up in it! Your brothers, they tried to rob the bank!"

"Yes, I know. Tim is back there. He will die soon. He believes I turned them in. I couldn't do it! I couldn't even shoot him!" Pete said in a strangled voice.

14

MIKE gave a sigh of relief as the train wheezed its way out of the station. He and Pete sat in a compartment that had two bunks which could be made up for sleeping. He had thought it an expense, but knew they both needed to sleep and to unwind. The last two hours in Flagstaff had been something of an ordeal. Just as they were loading their horses into a stock car, a man wearing buckskins, whom Mike had recognized as the one who'd been with the sheriff that night in the desert, had come brandishing a shotgun and had accused them of being connected with the outlaws. He had had to think quickly, giving Pete a nudge to stay quiet. The man had pointed to the roan. "I chased that one all the way to Arizona, and then I seen him in the mountains. There was another feller in a grey jacket, he rode him, then I seen you with a Mex up a valley."

Quickly, Mike had told him, "The outlaws stole the roan after they shot my cousin. When you came on me in the desert I was afraid to say anything in case you thought I was one of them. I still had to look for my cousin. You can see the sorrel is mine, I have the bill of sale."

Then Pete had shown the wound in his back, but the man still hadn't been convinced. "Where's his bill of sale?"

"He hasn't one because we bred and raised the roan in Montana," Mike lied, and Pete suppressed a smile.

Pete had said, "We had nothing to do with the Coltrains; and the Mexican, he helped me find them up in the mountains so I've been helping him move his sheep and goats to Sedona."

"The Coltrains? Is that who them varmints were?" the man had asked eagerly.

"Sure, we found out about them way back in Arizona. My cousin heard them talking after he took care of me."

"Yeah, that's right," Mike had interjected. "I had to take my cousin to the railroad, after I looked after his wound, then took the train to Holbrook. You've got no reason to insinuate we was with that scum," Mike had told the man, looking suitably angry.

Chandler had been thinking after hearing who the outlaws were, that there ought to be a decent reward for them, and then he'd remembered the mules tied in the trees west of town. He could claim them, too, if he got to them before anyone else did. Still flushed with success in catching the four men, and glad they were dead, he'd let them catch the train, and taken off in something of a hurry.

Mike sat watching the San Francisco Mountains disappear into the heavy cloud, then he turned to Pete. "Maybe we shouldn't have spent so much dough on the tickets."

"Listen, *amigo*. I have plenty of *dinero*. For years I saved what I stole from my pa and brothers. The men often paid me to do their laundry and look after their horses. They left money around when they were drunk and playing poker. I had a plan to save $10,000, then I would ride."

Mike grinned. "You'll have to mend your ways now. I have $620 now since you paid me for the bay, and I got a nice sum for the stallion and helping with the mustangs.

"We can get a few acres to grow what we need, and then try to catch some more mustangs. They say Utah is good, and north California. Arter we see the big water we'll head north apiece, see what we can find. It'll take a few years before we have a real place, but I'm through working for others, that's sure."

"Don't worry, Mike. Like I say, I have the *dinero* to buy us a good piece of land. $9,300 and some loose change ain't exactly small potatoes," Pete said, patting the small leather bag that hung round his neck on a thong under his shirt.

Mike stared. "Jumping jossifoots! I can't be your partner with my bit of chicken feed," he said disappointedly.

Pete looked unhappy at the stubborn expression on Mike's face, then he brightened.

"I buy us some cattle, you show me what to do. I don't know about these things. And you can put up something, and borrow some from me, I don't charge nothing. You pay it back when you want. That seems fair, don't it?"

Mike laughed, almost hysterically. "To think I might have rode right on by you in that desert, never even seen you, by God!"

"Then we're partners — *amigos*?"

"Sure, partners — *amigos*! Pass that damned bottle, let's do some celebrating!" Mike grinned.

FIGHTING RAMROD
Charles N. Heckelmann

Most men would have cut their losses, but Frazer counted the bullets in his guns and said he'd soak the range in blood before he'd give up another inch of what was his.

LONE GUN
Eric Allen

Smoke Blackbird had been away too long. The Lequires had seized the Blackbird farm, forcing the Indians and settlers off, and no one seemed willing to fight! He had to fight alone.

THE THIRD RIDER
Barry Cord

Mel Rawlins wasn't going to let anything stand in his way. His father was murdered, his two brothers gone. Now Mel rode for vengeance.

ARIZONA DRIFTERS
W. C. Tuttle

When drifting Dutton and Lonnie Steelman decide to become partners they find that they have a common enemy in the formidable Thurston brothers.

TOMBSTONE
Matt Braun

Wells Fargo paid Luke Starbuck to outgun the silver-thieving stagecoach gang at Tombstone. Before long Luke can see the only thing bearing fruit in this eldorado will be the gallows tree.

HIGH BORDER RIDERS
Lee Floren

Buckshot McKee and Tortilla Joe cut the trail of a border tough who was running Mexican beef into Texas. They stopped the smuggler in his tracks.

BRETT RANDALL, GAMBLER
E. B. Mann

Larry Day had the choice of running away from the law or of assuming a dead man's place. No matter what he decided he was bound to end up dead.

THE GUNSHARP
William R. Cox

The Eggerleys weren't very smart. They trained their sights on Will Carney and Arizona's biggest blood bath began.

THE DEPUTY OF SAN RIANO
Lawrence A. Keating and
Al. P. Nelson

When a man fell dead from his horse, Ed Grant was spotted riding away from the scene. The deputy sheriff rode out after him and came up against everything from gunfire to dynamite.

FARGO: MASSACRE RIVER
John Benteen

The ambushers up ahead had now blocked the road. Fargo's convoy was a jumble, a perfect target for the insurgents' weapons!

SUNDANCE: DEATH IN THE LAVA
John Benteen

The Modoc's captured the wagon train and its cargo of gold. But now the halfbreed they called Sundance was going after it . . .

HARSH RECKONING
Phil Ketchum

Five years of keeping himself alive in a brutal prison had made Brand tough and careless about who he gunned down . . .

FARGO: PANAMA GOLD
John Benteen

With foreign money behind him, Buckner was going to destroy the Panama Canal before it could be completed. Fargo's job was to stop Buckner.

FARGO:
THE SHARPSHOOTERS
John Benteen

The Canfield clan, thirty strong were raising hell in Texas. Fargo was tough enough to hold his own against the whole clan.

PISTOL LAW
Paul Evan Lehman

Lance Jones came back to Mustang for just one thing — revenge! Revenge on the people who had him thrown in jail.

HELL RIDERS
Steve Mensing

Wade Walker's kid brother, Duane, was locked up in the Silver City jail facing a rope at dawn. Wade was a ruthless outlaw, but he was smart, and he had vowed to have his brother out of jail before morning!

DESERT OF THE DAMNED
Nelson Nye

The law was after him for the murder of a marshal — a murder he didn't commit. Breen was after him for revenge — and Breen wouldn't stop at anything . . . blackmail, a frameup . . . or murder.

DAY OF THE COMANCHEROS
Steven C. Lawrence

Their very name struck terror into men's hearts — the Comancheros, a savage army of cutthroats who swept across Texas, leaving behind a bloodstained trail of robbery and murder.

SUNDANCE: SILENT ENEMY
John Benteen

A lone crazed Cheyenne was on a personal war path. They needed to pit one man against one crazed Indian. That man was Sundance.

LASSITER
Jack Slade

Lassiter wasn't the kind of man to listen to reason. Cross him once and he'll hold a grudge for years to come — if he let you live that long.

LAST STAGE TO GOMORRAH
Barry Cord

Jeff Carter, tough ex-riverboat gambler, now had himself a horse ranch that kept him free from gunfights and card games. Until Sturvesant of Wells Fargo showed up.

McALLISTER ON THE COMANCHE CROSSING
Matt Chisholm

The Comanche, McAllister owes them a life — and the trail is soaked with the blood of the men who had tried to outrun them before.

QUICK-TRIGGER COUNTRY
Clem Colt

Turkey Red hooked up with Curly Bill Graham's outlaw crew. But wholesale murder was out of Turk's line, so when range war flared he bucked the whole border gang alone . . .

CAMPAIGNING
Jim Miller

Ambushed on the Santa Fe trail, Sean Callahan is saved by two Indian strangers. But there'll be more lead and arrows flying before the band join Kit Carson against the Comanches.